THE AMOUNT TO CARRY

Also by Carter Scholz

Radiance
Kafka Americana (with Jonathan Lethem)
Palimpsests (with Glenn Harcourt)

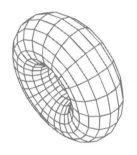

THE AMOUNT TO CARRY

stories by

CARTER SCHOLZ

PICADOR

NEW YORK

www.picadorusa.com

Book design by Jonathan Bennett

The following stories originally appeared, in somewhat different form, in these publications: "The Eve of the Last Apollo" in *Orbit 18,* "A Catastrophe Machine" in *The John W. Campbell Awards, vol. 5,* "Blumfeld, an Elderly Bachelor" in *Crank!,* "The Menagerie of Babel" in *Universe 14,* "A Draft of Canto CI" in *Afterlives,* "Altamira" in *The Magazine of Fantasy and Science Fiction,* "Travels" in *Isaac Asimov's SF Magazine,* "At the Shore" in *The Missouri Review,* "The Nine Billion Names of God" in *Light Years and Dark,* "Mengele's Jew" in *Starlight,* "The Amount to Carry" in *Starlight 2.*

ISBN 0-312-26901-3

First Edition: February 2003

10   9   8   7   6   5   4   3   2   1

For Barry N. Malzberg

CONTENTS

ACKNOWLEDGMENTS

I wish to thank all the editors who were generous to me with more than just their pages: Damon Knight, Kate Wilhelm, Terry Carr, Robert Silverberg, Ed Ferman, Gardner Dozois, Marta Randall, Ellen Datlow, George R. R. Martin, Scott Edelman, Chris Drumm, Michael Bishop, Pamela Sargent, Ian Watson, Beth Meacham, Bryan Cholfin, Greg Bear, Patrick Nielsen Hayden, Robert Killheffer.

THE AMOUNT TO CARRY

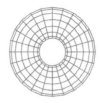

THE EVE OF THE LAST APOLLO

MILESTONES

DIED. JOHN Christie Andrews, 64, U.S. Air Force (Brig. Gen., ret.); of a heart attack. Born July 17, 1935 in Abilene, Texas, Andrews was commander of the first manned spacecraft to land on the Moon. He is survived by a wife and son.

No. I don't like that dream.

The dream-magazine faded and he was back in 1975, tentatively at least, until sleep plucked him again into a land beyond life where his existence could be reduced to those two dates: his achievement and his death.

The curtains ballooned inward on a light breeze. He caught at them, and saw the moon standing in the sky. It was gibbous, bloated past half but less than full. He hated it like that, the lopsidedness of it. Half or full or crescent he could stand some nights, but there was nothing tolerable in a gibbous moon. He could not pick out within five hundred miles the place on its surface where he had walked, just five years ago.

No cars passed on State Street. The moon might have been another street lamp. From his present vantage point in Teaneck, New Jersey, it seemed impossible that he had ever been there.

———

The Lunar Exposé. Time magazine, *August 2, 1987.* The article
explained that the moon landing had been a hoax, since the
moon itself was a hoax. It explained how simple it had been for
unknown forces to simulate the moon for unscrupulous pur-
poses. A conspiracy of poets and scientists was intimated. Mass
hypnosis was mentioned. In a sidebar was a capsule summary
of his alleged mission with a drawing of the flight path, the
complicated loops and curves that had taken them there and
back, straight-line flight being impossible in space, with an inset
map of the splashdown area. Suddenly he was in the capsule as
it splashed, sank, and bobbed to the surface. He wanted to fling
the hatch open and yell in triumph, be dazzled by the spray and
brilliant blue Pacific sky, but of course he couldn't do that, there
was no telling what germs they had brought back, what germs
had survived the billion-year killing lunar cold and void, and
the helicopters droned down and netted them and swung them
to the carrier and into quarantine and for three weeks they saw
people only through glass; that may have been the start of the
isolation he felt now, just as his first time in space had been the
start of the emptiness. When he had reached the Cape after all
those weeks and miles and loops and backtracks, the trip was
finally over, and he yielded to an impulse; he walked onto the
launching pad and bent to put his hand on the scorched
ground—but he had an attack of vertigo and a terrible inti-
mation: the Earth itself had moved. If he went to the Cape
exactly a year after the liftoff, the Earth would be in position
again, the circle would be closed—but then there was the motion of the solar system through the galaxy to consider, and the
sweep of the galaxy through the universe, and the universe's
own pulsations—and he saw there was no way for him ever to
close the circle and return to the place he started from. Driving
home with the road behind him spiraling off through space as
the Earth moved and the Sun moved and the galaxy moved,

he became ill and had to pull off the road. Only when it grew dark was he able to drive again, slowly.

The dream, the memory, dissolved.

By the time he woke next morning his wife had already left to spend another weekend at the commune upstate. He made breakfast for himself and his son and went outside in the Saturday morning heat to garden. He was almost forty.

He worked in an over-airconditioned building adjacent to the Teaneck Armory. On one wall of his office was a maroon and red square of geometrically patterned fabric framed like a painting. On another was an autographed photo of the President and another photo of himself on the moon; the landing module and his crewmate Jirn Cooper were reflected in his face mask. Because it was a NASA publicity photo, his autograph was on it. He felt silly about that and had always meant to get a clean copy, but where he worked now there were no NASA photos.

After he had walked on the moon and declined promotion to an Air Force base in California, they seemed to have run out of things for him to do. He had a wood veneer desk that was generally clean and empty. On the floor was a cheap red carpet, the nap of which he was always carrying home on his shoes.

At first after the mission his time had been filled with interviews and tours and banquets and inconveniences, but with time his fame dwindled. At first he welcomed this escape from the public eye; then the emptiness began to weigh on him, like a column of air on his shoulders. The time he could now spend with his wife and son passed uneasily. He learned to play golf and tennis and spent more time at them than he enjoyed. He started a diary and grew depressed with the banality of his life.

So in the summer of 1975 he found himself sorting the fragments of his life: his wife's absence, the imminent end of his

fourth four-year term of service in the Air Force, the dead un-
dying image of the moon that haunted his dreams, the book he
had long planned to write, the mystery of his son, the possibility
of a life ahead without a wife or son or career or public image,
without every base he had come to rely on. He felt he had to
consider what he was, and what he might become.

For a project he started a garden, even though it was the
height of summer. He hauled sacks of soil amendments in the
station wagon, rented a rototiller, chewed up part of the back-
yard, sweated through his t-shirt and shorts. Each day the heat
seemed to come down on him sooner and harder. Each day he
would hear Kevin go out, and then he would go back into the
silent empty house to rest.

The lunar astronauts, the dozen or so people he had considered
friends, drifted one by one away from the magnet of Houston,
until the terrible clean emptiness of the city came to depress
him. Texas no longer felt like home.

In 1970 Harrison Baker, the command module pilot on Andrews's mission, moved to New Jersey with his family to become a vice-president in a large oil company. The Andrewses
followed shortly. The prospect of friends nearby, and of New
York, where he and Charlotte had once wanted to live, Kevin's
enthusiasm for leaving Texas, all these poor random factors
pulled them to the sterile suburb of Teaneck as surely as destiny.
As it turned out, they ended over forty miles from the Bakers,
New York lost its appeal after six months, and Kevin talked of
going back to Texas for college.

Baker had written a book on what it was like to orbit the
moon while his fellow astronauts got all the glory. The book
was called *Group Effort*. A bad book, Andrews thought. A hum-
ble book by a conceited man, written in fact by a hungry young
journalist. Andrews had the impression, reading it, that Baker

was somehow unconvinced of the Moon's reality, since he himself had not walked there. Andrews disliked the book, or more
precisely he disliked the feelings the book aroused in him: he
felt he could have done it better if he had made the effort.

But adrift in this summer he nonetheless called Baker one
day. He was alone in the house and desperate for company. He
called him as if to summon a ghost of old confidence.

"Chris! How are you, you son of a bitch?" Baker's voice was
hard and distant on the wire. Andrews had quite forgotten that
at NASA Chris had been his nickname. He had also forgotten
Baker's smiling combativeness, his way of wielding friendship
like a challenge. Already he was regretting the call.

"Hello, Hank. How are you?"

"Great, just great! Listen, I've been meaning to invite you
and Sharl up for a weekend. It's been too long."

"Fine. Thanks, Hank. But actually Charlotte and I haven't
been getting on too well recently."

"Oh? I'm sorry to hear it."

"It's just one of those things. We're thinking of separating."

"That's a shame, Chris. That's a damn shame. Francie and I
always said what a good couple you were."

"Well, I don't know, I think it's for the best. Hell, I didn't
call to cry on your shoulder, Hank. I had a question for you.
I've been thinking of writing that book that Doubleday asked
me to, you remember?"

"Sure. They're still interested?"

"Well, I don't know. I assumed they would be."

"It's been a few years, hasn't it? You know, the royalties on
my book aren't what they could be. The hardcover's out of
print and the paperback sales are so slow they're not going to
reprint it. Which is a damn shame, I think. Not that I need the
money. But the way I feel about it is, it's a historical document
and it ought to stay in print. But they say people aren't interested in the moon anymore. People don't care."

"Well, sure, look at the whole NASA program."

"Well, I'm a retired guy now. I don't really follow the program."

"This is the last one, Hank. The one coming up. After this, no more manned flights."

There was silence. He remembered Baker's habit of keeping him waiting on the line, when Baker was in the orbiter.

"Hank? I can't help thinking we did it wrong."

"Wrong? What do you mean?"

"Our landing. We planted the American flag, we left a plaque."

"So? What should we have planted? Flowers?" Baker laughed, a short cold sound in the receiver.

"I don't know. I thought the United Nations flag might have been a nice gesture."

"The UN? What's the UN done for you lately? We put that lander on the moon. Why shouldn't we take the credit for it?"

"I suppose. I didn't think much about it at the time." The flag would not unfurl in vacuum so they had braced it with wire.

"What's to think about? I mean, this is off the record, this isn't a damn NASA press release, but that flag marks our territory. I don't care what the plaque said about coming in peace for all mankind. We got there before the Russians did. It's that simple."

"What about the joint Apollo-Soyuz mission coming up?"

"Well, shit. There's a good reason to be out of NASA right there. The Russians get more out of it than we do. You want my take on it, we'll have a manned program again, Chris, yes we will. But it won't be NASA. We'll take space back from those fucking civilians. Mark my words. Now, Chris, I got to run. Some big shot wants to buy me lunch, get me to sit on a board somewhere. That invitation still goes for you and your kid, and for Charlotte if you want. Any time at all, you know that."

"Sure, Hank. Thanks."

"I hope it all works out for you."

"I'm sure it will. I'll let you go. Good talking to you."

"See you around, huh?"

"You bet." He hung up. He felt very tired. The living room trembled just outside his field of vision. He sat for a few minutes, and abruptly decided to spend the day in New York, in noise and smog and traffic.

Through the magazine where she worked, his wife had met an author who ran a commune in upstate New York. The author had published an article on communal lifestyles in the magazine. Charlotte brought it home, and Andrews read it with disdain. A few weeks later the author dropped by the office in person and talked to Charlotte. She came home excited, with an invitation to the commune for both of them, which, after a week of bitter arguments, she accepted alone. She would sleep with the author; of that Andrews was sure. And when she came home Andrews said, stupidly, regretting it even as he spoke, "Was he any good?"

And she said, "He was great," and what had been a bitterness became a war. During a lull in the fight they heard Kevin sobbing through the wall.

"My God," said Charlotte, "what's wrong with us?" Together they went to Kevin, and the three of them held to each other and wept.

The next month was perhaps the best in their marriage; they were kind and deferential, as if unwilling to test the strength of the frayed fabric. But the next time Charlotte left it was for a week. Again there was a fight. Again there were tears. After that, the reconciliations had less meaning. Andrews felt the marriage become weak and brittle, emulsion cracking on an old photograph.

The black and white photograph in the den held them both against a bright, faded Texas sky. They stood by a small brick chapel in the hot Texas afternoon, Charlotte in her crisp white dress, four months pregnant but not yet showing, Andrews crewcut and stiff in his uniform. Andrews had entered the Air Force from college, blank enough to be a soldier, smart enough to be an officer. Soon he had commendations, citations, and his name on a plastic wood-grained prism on his desk at Sheppard Air Force Base and $213.75 a month plus expenses. Everything fell into place. He had a wife and a master's degree and a mortgage, and a son, and then a doctorate and oak leaves and an assured future.

Then the space program started up, and Lieutenant Colonel Andrews, a local boy of good repute, an officer and an engineer and a test pilot, and a solid asset to any organization, so it said on his commendations, was accepted into those elite ranks. He got his colonelcy and a sense of purpose that truly humbled him; he had never been religious but space made him feel as he imagined God made other people feel. He was a successful man, and his life was a fine and balanced thing.

Then they put him in a rocket and shot him at the moon.

Abenezra, Abulfeda, Agatharchides, Agrippa, Albategnius, Alexander, Aliacensis, Almanon, Alpetragius, Alphonsus, Apianus, Apollonius, Arago, Archimedes, Aristarchus, Aristillus, Aristoteles, Asclepi, Atlas . . .

The craters, the names, rolled past. A tiny motor made a grinding sound as it turned the four-foot sphere, the front and back sides both sculpted in wondrous detail thanks to his and other missions, thanks to the automatic cameras mounted on the outside of the capsule. Tiny American flags marked the Apollo landing sites, dime-store gaudies against the gray.

John Christie Andrews, first man on the moon, stood in the planetarium at the end of a hall lined with names like Icarus, da Vinci, Montgolfier, Wright, Goddard inscribed over a mural of the history of flight. They had told him that the moon landing was the grandest achievement of the human race. He believed it was. He had every reason to be proud, to be as content as Baker seemed to be. Why, then, did that emptiness come to him at night?

Flanking the lunar globe were photographs: himself, Baker, Cooper, Nixon, von Braun. Some children recognized him and crowded around for autographs. One asked where he had landed; again he suffered doubts and finally stabbed a finger vaguely at one of the larger maria. Gratefully he heard the loudspeaker announce the start of the sky show.

The sky show was absorbing, more so than the night sky, even the clear country sky at his brother-in-law's summer cottage on Lake Hopatcong; he was enchanted by the flitting arrows on the sky, the narrator's calm clear explanations, the wonderful control the projector had over its model universe. Stars rose, set, went forward, back. Seasons fled and returned. In the planetarium, time did not exist.

Afterwards he walked along the edge of Central Park. In a bookstore window he saw a copy of Baker's book, marked down to $1.98. He went in. Near the entrance his eye was caught by a familiar volume, an anthology of poetry he had used in college. He stood there skimming it. *The moon is dead, you lovers . . . I have seen her face . . . a woman's face but dead as stone. And leper white and withered to the bone . . .*

He saw Charlotte's face deflagrate before him. Touched by the void, it turned into a death's-head moon, glowing with the stark brilliance of sunlight in void. Something struggled in his chest. It seemed to Andrews that of all the astronauts, he had had the best chance of understanding the moon. Of what they had done there. He would write his book. Why not? And he would start it with poetry.

He purchased the anthology, and several others. It was years since he had read anything but newspapers; now he was drunk with the neglected mysteries of books. In this nearly weightless mood he felt himself approaching the edge of a change, the crest of an oscillation, the start of a new phase; he felt charged with the energy of the unpredictable.

"Dad? You busy?"

He started and pushed aside the books he had bought. "Oh, no. Come on in, son." Immediately annoyed at himself; when had he started calling Kevin son?

The boy drifted in. Tall, pale; his son, brought out of a hot union years past, and already faded, but for this phantom, this stranger in the house. His son.

"Are you and Mom going to stay together?"

"Sure. Until you're at college."

"Oh." The room was silent. Somewhere an air conditioner hummed.

"Why do you ask?"

"Things are worse between you, aren't they?"

"Don't worry about it, Kevin."

"If you're staying together just for my sake, I wish you wouldn't. I mean, I don't want you to. I think you should separate now if that's the case."

Andrews looked at his son. His emotions already burnt brittle into a fragile, ashen maturity. While Andrews felt himself moving back along a rocket wake into a second adolescence, a time of self-consciousness, self-discovery.

"I'll think about it. I'll talk to your mother. Kevin . . . ?"

"Yeah, Dad."

"This business with your mother and me . . . it hasn't affected you too badly, has it?" He burned with embarrassment. His memory stung him brutally with the image of a woman he had, just once, brought to the house, out of spite for Charlotte and her author, and Kevin's look when he came home. "I mean, just because things aren't working out for us, I don't want you to think . . ."

"I don't think about it anymore. It's just one of those things that happen."

"Because it would be a terrible thing if this were to turn you against marriage, or against women . . ."

"Don't worry about it, Dad. I think it's better this way. I think it might even be better for you if you split up sooner."

"Well, thanks, Kev." Then, because he was less afraid of being embarrassed than of being untouchable, he hugged his son. Kevin held still for this, and Andrews let go soon enough to make both of them grateful.

"Okay if I stay out late tonight?" Kevin asked a few minutes later, as he was leaving. "I have a date."

"How late?" Pleased, but their late sentiment demanded a strict return to formality. The balance was too delicate to threaten.

"One o'clock?"

"Make it twelve-thirty."

"Okay."

"Who's the girl?"

"Nobody you know."

"Oh. Well . . . have fun . . ."

Kevin left. Andrews returned to his book and read: *Poetry must bring forth its characters as speaking, singing, gesticulating. This is the nature of the hero.* He put the book down and stared dumbly into space.

His obligations as a national monument took him the next day to a half-hour talk show with a senator, a NASA administrator, and a moderator. The end of the manned space program had been made topical by the upcoming Apollo-Soyuz mission.

The show started with the senator asserting that the space program was by no means ending, but was being cut back in favor of more pressing domestic issues. The senator said that space exploration could be done more cheaply and efficiently and safely by machines. Andrews felt that he was being mollified, and this increased his hostility. He interrupted to ask if perhaps other areas of the national budget might be better cut— defense, for instance, which consumed a hundred times as much money as NASA.

No one knew how to react; Andrews thought the NASA man might be smiling, off-camera. The senator made some comment about his record for trimming waste, and the moderator turned the conversation toward the hopeful symbolism of the joint Apollo-Soyuz mission. The senator, recovered, called it a magnificent extension of his party's successful policy of détente. Andrews began to ask why, if détente was so successful, the defense budget was not being cut, but as he leaned forward to press his point, he realized that his microphone was off and the camera had moved away from him. This so angered him that he leaned into the camera's view and began to speak into the senator's microphone.

"I'd like to read something, if you don't mind."

The camera swung back to him. The lights blazed and blinded him. He felt a little drunk with their heat.

"This is a poem by Lord Byron. It's very short."

The paper trembled in his hand.

"So, we'll go no more a-roving
So late into the night,
Though the heart be still as loving,
And the moon be still as bright.
For the sword outwears its sheath,
And the soul wears out the breast.
And the heart must pause to breathe,
And love itself have rest.
Though the night was made for loving,
And the day returns too soon,
Yet we'll go no more a-roving
By the light of the moon."

Electrons made a chaos of snow on the monitors. Offstage a man in hornrimmed glasses waved frantically. The moderator cleared his throat.

"Thank you, Colonel Andrews. We have to pause here, but we'll be back in a moment." The red eye of the camera blinked off.

Andrews sank back into his chair. The senator looked away. The moderator leaned over to Andrews and said, "Please, Colonel, stick to the subject at hand."

"Wasn't I?"

"Colonel . . ."

"My microphone was turned off. It made me mad."

"I'll see it doesn't happen again. But please . . ."

"No more poetry?"

"No more poetry."

Andrews turned to the NASA man, his silent ally, who said, "This isn't helping us, Colonel," and his certainty vanished. NASA itself did not care about the moon. Andrews was alone in his concern.

"All right," he said under his breath. "All right, you bastards." He felt a sense of climax. He saw what he must do: leave, walk off, now. He had said all he had to say. But at the thought all his strength went from him. The camera came back on, and for the rest of the show he was trapped there, silent, outwardly serene. He saw himself swimming alone and untouched in a sea of static.

Tuesday his wife returned. The car pulled up and he heard Kevin go down and out the back door, fast and light, as if he had been going anyway. The screen door sighed on its hinge and in the second before she entered the den he knew with a sick premonition that today she would finally ask for a divorce. Her first words, though, catching him off balance, were, "My God, John, do you have any idea how embarrassing that was?"

"Hello, Charlotte. What was embarrassing?" He considered the woman before him with an objectivity he would never have thought possible.

"The TV show. The poetry. Rick practically dragged the whole commune in to watch you quoting Lord Byron on the *Today* show. Christ, if you knew what you looked like."

"Really. I didn't know you had TV up there in the pristine wilderness."

"Oh, go screw."

"All right, let's have it, what was wrong with quoting Byron?"

"It was, let us say, out of character."

"Did it ever occur to you that I get tired of playing the dumb hero?"

She looked at him. "You think you can get out of it that easily?"

"Maybe."

She went to her bedroom and took down a suitcase from the closet. He followed her and sat on the bed with his eyes closed and his fingertips touching at the bridge of his nose. He sat as if in another world and listened to the angry rustlings of clothes as she hurled them about.

"Tell me, John, do you have any idea the kind of crap I have had to put up with these past ten years?"

"Yes." It had once been a joke between them.

"The goddamned forty-page NASA manual on how to be an astronaut's wife? Did you get a good look at that?"

"Charlotte, don't start."

"John."

"Yes," he said.

"John, I want a divorce."

"Yes, I know. All right."

"All right? Like that?"

"Like that."

She stared, confused. "What are you going to do?"

"I don't know."

"Your term of service is over this month, isn't it? Are you going to renew?"

"I don't think so."

"Why not?" She sat on the bed now and he became aware of her body, her movements, and it began to hurt. He had held it off till then. "What are you going to do for money? Another four years and you'd have a pension. Kevin will be in college. If you quit now, what will you do?"

"I was thinking of writing a book."

"About your mission?"

"Sort of. I was thinking of poetry."

"Poetry?" She smiled fractionally and shook her head. "Lover, if you had the barest fraction of poetry in you, it would have come out long ago. You would have said something full of poetry when you first stepped onto the moon. And what did you say? Well, I don't have to remind you."

"Those were their words, not mine."

She shook her head wearily. "John, it's too late. It's five years too late. You can't be what you're not. You're, what did you say, a national monument. As soon as you touched that rock up there you turned to stone yourself. I know, because I almost did too. I came so damned close to it, but I . . ." She stopped herself.

"Go on."

She looked up quickly. "You want me to?"

"Yes."

She paused. She looked at her hands. "While you were on the moon I seduced a newsman."

"Say that again."

"I seduced a newsman. You didn't know that, did you?"

"No, Charlotte, I didn't know that." He felt a dull ache start, a sinking at the truth of it, or at her ability to lie that way. "I don't know when to believe you anymore."

"You can believe this. It was right after you'd stepped down. He was here to interview me, to ask me safe dull questions for his safe dull article. Kevin was at school, you were a quarter million miles away; so we did it. It was the safest infidelity I ever had."

"Meaning there were others."

"Meaning whatever you like."

Feeling was returning to him; he had tried to hold it off, but the dull ache was deep in his spine.

"And right after we finished the phone rang. He looked like it was the voice of God. I said, 'Oh, that's just my husband calling from work,' and I laughed! I felt so fine! Isn't that funny, that I didn't have to worry about you walking in on us because you were on the moon?"

He got up and left the room. "John," she called. He kept walking. He walked into the kitchen to get a beer, the feeling still in his spine. When he reached the refrigerator there was a roaring in his ears. Cold air blew out across his arms; he stared into the cluttered recess of milk, butter, eggs, foilwrapped leftovers. His mind was blank. Finally he remembered about the beer and reached for it. He was shocked to see his hand shake as it lifted the bottle. He put the bottle carefully back and shut the door, stood braced against it. His back throbbed. When it subsided he walked back to the bedroom. "Why?" he said.

Charlotte watched him. "Because, John, I was slightly drunk and terribly depressed because there was my husband on the moon, and where was he? I felt nothing. I felt like a piece of machinery for the goddamned mission and I had to do something human for Christ's sake, can you understand that?"

"That wasn't human. That was sick and vindictive."

"I watched you on the moon, John, I watched the whole thing. I wanted so much to share your moment, and I couldn't. It meant nothing. It wasn't real to me. You said their words, you followed their agenda, you did nothing, nothing, to show that you were my husband. I watched you become NASA, and I was the NASA wife. And I felt like I was dying. And here was this reporter saying, 'You must be awfully proud, Mrs. Andrews.' And you moved like a robot on the moon and I did not want to be married to that! So I fucked him. I did it, and I made him think of me as a person!" And she laughed in triumph and looked at him quickly as she used to, when the life and the devilry in her was for him only. The look caught at him and something seemed to break free from her eyes and fly, and something twisted inside him, watching it go.

"Charlotte . . ." His mouth was dry and his voice came from far away. "Stay with me."

"No."

"Yes." He was pleading. "Yes."

"Why should I, John?"

"I need you. Kevin needs you."

For a second she was moved, he saw it; her eyes softened and she seemed to tremble with the thought of going to him, there was that ghost of a better past between them for an instant.

She seemed ready to cry, but with an effort she turned to him and forced her tears back to whatever pit they had been rising from; she fixed him with dry glittering eyes that said no; I am not that close to you.

"John, I have needs too," she said.

Numb, he followed her to the car, helped her with her bags. She got in, started the engine, and stared straight ahead for a minute before turning to him.

"You could come visit me," she said.

There was a long silence. "I don't think so. I'd better be alone."

And she drove off. That it was inevitable, that he had seen it coming for months, that his every nerve was raw with waiting for it, made no difference to the wretched man who now stands and watches a woman who had been his wife vanish down the road.

He has a dream that first night after she has finally left. It is one of many in the blurry confused time before waking. He is lying on his back with an erection while a woman pulls herself onto him. When he fucks his wife this way, as he often does at her prompting, he puts his hands to her breasts or on her hips, but in this dream he can't move. His arms stay limp at his sides. The woman is moving, though, sliding on him, and he remembers that in space his wet dreams were usually of women masturbating. This dream-woman seems to be doing that now; he feels like a machine for her pleasure—and it's good to feel that, to give himself over to her pleasure, to abandon his responsibilities.

As he wakes further, the dream fades and he realizes that the sheet is tented over him and the slightest move will bring him off. He lies still. Only the fractional pull of the sheet as he breathes can be felt, with almost unbearable friction. Finally he turns onto his stomach and pumps himself into the sheet, reliving agonies of adolescence, twice this week I sinned father, it was that that drove him from the Church. He lies for some time, feeling himself pulse, and grow damp and cold.

Alone, becalmed, he had books to read and silence in which to think and money enough to last the summer, a quiet season of the soul that seemed timeless. But it passed. His reenlistment forms came; Kevin was preparing for college; he had to grow used to the idea of divorce. The house took on a dull dead feel, as if his eyes in passing over objects too many times had burnt the life from them. He felt beyond continuing. He found a line in Yeats that pierced him with its truth: Man is in love, and loves what vanishes.

So for a week or two he worked at trying to find in his unwilling soul the shape of a book that would say what he felt about the moon. He copied poems from his anthology. He reread Baker's book. The event was too familiar; even as he rehearsed it in his mind, he could feel the particularity of it slipping away from him. Instead he jotted fragments based on moments he remembered: earthrise over the crescent limb while they still orbited the moon at eighty miles; the feel of the light gravity; the way the lunar dust burst from underfoot, hung and drifted. He wrote short paragraphs, sometimes just fragments of sentences that looked like lines of poetry. He typed up what he had and clipped a cover letter to the pages, hoping his name would make up for their defects.

Then, emptied, he called his wife at the number she had left. When he heard her voice he sickened and softened inside and was near tears when he asked to come up and see her and she said, she says, yes.

———————

On the drive up he is tense with anticipation. His pulse is up, his chest tight, his breathing shallow, almost as if he is in a capsule again. He admits to himself that some of this is fear. Not of Charlotte or her author, but of the commune. The young people there. He sees teenaged girls drifting through the Teaneck summer. He is more disconcerted by them than Kevin is. To find himself at that age he would have to go back to Waco, 1951—and for an instant it seems possible—exit 12 for the McCarthy hearings, exit 13 for the Korean War—it seems he could return to his youth as easily as he now drives the Thruway. But it would not be the youth of these new children. This generation seems astute, mature beyond their years, beyond perhaps his.

The commune is not what he expected. No farmhouse, no wide furrowed fields, no cows or sheep grazing. It is a modest two-story home surrounded by neatly pruned shrubs. In a small garden he sees a man about his age shade his eyes to watch his car lurch up the dirt drive. This is the author, no doubt. The man sets down his hoe and approaches.

"I'm Rick Burns. You must be Colonel Andrews. Charlotte told us to expect you."

He is drained from the trip; the sun hits him a blow as he climbs out of the air-conditioned car. He shakes hands, feeling the man's grip, feeling it as if it were on his wife.

"Come inside. We're glad you decided to come up."

He dislikes Burns on sight, his bluff cordiality, the veneer of sexuality on the man's skin like a deep tan.

The only person inside is Charlotte, crosslegged on the sofa, reading. She looks up when Andrews enters; she has heard the car and arranged herself purposely into that neutral position, and stays seated, realizing that a hug would be too intimate, a handshake too cold. In his consideration of adolescence, in his high pitch of sexual awareness, all he can think of is how much he has missed her physically.

Charlotte rises. "I'll show John around."

"Dinner's late tonight, around nine."

They go out; they speak little. She tells him there are half a dozen young people living here, working and paying what they can. Rick bears most of the expense. There is a small barn behind the house, hens, a couple of pigs, turkeys, ducks. Charlotte says hello to a couple, Robert and Barbara, as they emerge from the barn, smiling with slight embarrassment. Andrews looks at Charlotte, squeezes her hand. And soon enough they end up back in her bedroom.

He steps outside himself and observes them both there in the waning light. Charlotte unbuttons her blue shirt and the sun is gold and shadow on her. The room is vivid in oranges and browns. Even Andrews's large body, going to fat from lack of training, is handsome in the twilight. He lies naked on the bed, the sheets cool, the air gentle, Charlotte sliding silken over him. Her breasts glow pale against her tan. She moves onto him as in his dream; he is still as death, as in the dream; and suddenly he thrusts against her. She puts a hand to his chest to slow him, but he moves again, frantic now to break the spell of dream that seems to hover close. She presses harder, and furious, he grabs her shoulders and wrenches her over with a small gasp under him, pumping desperately, starting a rhythm, a continuity, a feeling that in these seconds, these thrusts, he can vindicate all their time passed and gone sour.

Perhaps she understands then, or perhaps her body betrays her, or perhaps she has reasons of her own, but she moves in sympathy; she gives Andrews his dominance. Gives it just as Andrews softens. He comes up off her and rolls away and lies still, hardly breathing.

"John, it doesn't matter. It's all right."

"No. No, it isn't."

"Shh. Yes. It is. I don't care."

Andrews lies quietly as she caresses him. And peace comes like grace; what a wonder, to have his wife back as she was, even for these few moments. Dusk gathers, and he has visions of space, at once appealing and terrifying. The world releases him, and he soars transcendent through the firmament. After a while the stars resolve to the grainy darkness of the room and Charlotte is beside him and they talk.

"What is it you want here, Sharl?"

"I don't know if I can explain. It's a feeling. It's as if I've spent my whole life inside, in some horrible hospital or rest home. I haven't felt really free since God knows when. I feel pale and bedridden. I just want to feel healthy again."

"Yes," he says. "Sometimes I feel the air pressing on me. I feel gravity and I feel the atmosphere like an ocean on my back. And I want to be in free fall again. I dream about that sometimes."

"This is what NASA is to you?"

"Was."

"Why do you want to resign, then?"

"Because it's over! Didn't you hear me on that program? It's over, done, finished." He groans and rolls away from her. "It could have been something and we let it go. What sense does that make?"

"John," she soothes, holding him. Against the coldness of space, the transcendent spirit of man, her warmth is cloying. She binds him to his body. "What's out there, anyway?"

"Nothing," he says, and he shuts his eyes.

On an ocean. Wave mechanics. Harmonic motion. His physics professor, strange old man, explaining the motion of the waves: periodic functions, series of crests and troughs, repetitions. Every sort of motion depends upon harmonic theory. Sine waves, circles, spirals, helixes, orbits, all the same. Period of a pendulum. Earth's a pendulum, you know: swings around the sun, and turns on its axis: complex motion. The brilliant mind derailed and rambling as the classroom pitched on the waves: duality in monism, one wave with the two halves, see? Positive and negative. Mathematics is the purest poetry. Ah, the Greeks, such poets. Class grumbling, breaking up and diving off the platform, old fool senile and rambling about sine fucking waves. Sit down! I'm not finished! Andrews alone in the classroom. Now listen, hissed the teacher, air seething with his hot intense breath, the sea growing long and glassy as if listening. We are all disturbances of the medium. Understand? Disturbances of the medium. Pebbles dropped in a vacuum. Waves. All of us, a collection of waves, nothing more. Nothing but repetitions, periods, waves. Frightened, Andrews dove, sank quickly, drowned, and drowning, woke.

As he enters the kitchen and faces all the members of the commune together for dinner, he feels lines of force in the room, constellations of tensions shifting to accommodate him. Interference patterns. How distant he is from this world; how far away Teaneck is. The others feel this too, and there is that moment of uneasiness, the lines in flux. The moment passes. They sit to dinner.

The dinner conversation ranges over books, music, films, farming. One girl casually mentions her abortion and Andrews suffers a Catholic reaction. Not that he has been at all religious, but a sense of sin, once acquired, is not easily lost. Sin and grace are not part of the metaphysical baggage of this generation. They speak of yin and yang, complementaries without values. He feels at a loss, vulnerable.

After dinner they sit and talk over the littered plates. Burns starts to roll a cigarette. He has rolled several from tobacco that evening, but now he reaches for a smaller jar, and the flakes are green and Andrews feels a kick of giddy trepidation as he watches Burns pour the stuff into a paper and roll it. He is acutely aware of everyone, of their casualness and his tension, and he feels Charlotte watching him. The joint circles around, closing on him. Charlotte tokes, smiles at him, and passes it. He shakes his head. She nods and smiles, makes "come on" with her mouth. Afraid of interrupting the casual atmosphere, afraid of making a scene, afraid perhaps of missing a chance, he accepts, sucks, holds, passes. "Keep it in," Charlotte whispers. He nods secretly. John Andrews, pothead.

At first he feels nothing and starts to relax, but after a while a certain detachment slips into his senses. They extend; his eyes, ears, fingers are at the far end of a tunnel, relaying everything to him in delayed echoes. Everything has flattened, taken on the aspect of a screen. Entranced, Andrews watches as he would in a theater. Colors are rich, vivid, the dialogue flows wondrously. How lifelike, he thinks.

This goes on for some time before a young man named Max gets up. Andrews runs the scene back: Burns has asked how many chickens he can expect for dinner tomorrow and Max said, "I'll go out and cull some now. Come on, Barb." Then he senses Andrews's gaze. "Want to see how you cull chickens, Colonel?" and Andrews, suffused with good will, says, "Why, shore," and they are up and out.

There is silence outside, a breathless summer silence, with a full moon, orange, just rising. On the horizon fireworks burst soundlessly. The Fourth, Andrews suddenly remembers. It is the Fourth of July. America is 199 tonight.

In the barn is a rich earth shit smell. In the roost the birds flutter and cluck at the flashlight. Max says, "We have a dozen birds but we're only getting about eight eggs a day. So we must have a couple hens not doing their jobs." He lifts a brown hen which squawks indignantly. Barb takes the light. The hen's eyes gleam yellow and she squirms. "Down," says Max. "Keep it out of her eyes, Barb."

He carries the bird into the adjoining shed, away from the others, and snaps on the light. He says to Andrews, "Now the first thing you do is check the claws. If the hen's not laying, the yellow pigment that should go into the yolk gets into the beak and claws and around the vent." He turns the hen over and she squawks. "Pretty good. Now you check the vent." He pushes the tail feathers aside and a pink puckered hole appears. "It should be moist and bleached—no yellow—and this one looks pretty good." Abruptly Max lays his fingers beside the vent. "Check the pelvic bone for clearance, make sure the eggs have room to get out." He flips the hen back rightside up. "Yeah, she looks like a layer. Give her a white tag, Barb." The girl has a handful of colored plastic rings. Now she snaps a white one around the bird's horny leg. Max takes the hen back in, emerges with another. "When they stop laying," he says, "they start looking a lot better. The muscles firm up and the feathers get slicker. So I get very suspicious when I see a healthy-looking bird like this one." He flips her over. The hen thrashes wildly, flaps the air with frantic wings. "Oh, baby," says Max, "you're much too active. You're looking too good to be spending much time in the laying box." He holds her firmly. "Vent looks okay, though. Two fingers here. . . . Give her a yellow, Barb."

After eleven hens there is only one cull, a red tag already in a separate cage. Max brings in the last bird. "This is a sex-linked. I would be very surprised if she wasn't laying. Still, you can never tell. The only way you find out for sure is to kill it and check the egg tree. I killed a cull once that had an egg all ready to drop out. Ate the chicken, fried the egg. But we lost a layer. And they moult in July and they don't lay while they're moulting. Every poultry book I've ever read says, come July, you can forget about eggs."

As soon as Max starts poking, the bird explodes in frenzy. The claws kick, the wings flail. Max puts a hand on the bird's neck. "If you choke 'em a little, it calms 'em." The hen does not calm though and Max shifts her further upside down. A claw catches his shirt. "Shit!" He drops the hen and Barb grabs her. "You hurt?" "No. Just a scratch." She holds the bird while Max probes. He spreads the feathers to show Andrews the dry tight yellow vent. "Ahh." Max lifts her, calm now, and drops her in the cage with the other cull. She flutters once and is still.

He smiles at Andrews.

"Dinner."

When they come back to the house, Andrews is still high, still enchanted with the world. But something has changed inside. One of the girls gives him a quick look, then goes back to her book. Andrews sweeps his eyes slowly around the room. He says, "Where's my wife?" No one answers.

He pauses for only a second as he reaches his wife's door—the hairs on his wrists move and his hand stops before touching the knob—then he twists, pushes.

Charlotte is sitting on the bed with Burns. Burns has both of her hands in his and he is leaning to kiss her. Before Burns can rise, Andrews has pulled him to his feet. He hits him in the stomach. Burns gasps with astonishment and Andrews hits him again. Charlotte spits, "Bastard!" and grabs at his arms. Andrews can feel the rhythm of it, he is hurting Burns, hear him grunt, but Charlotte is pushing him back and Burns is rising with his hands outstretched. "Stop it!" Charlotte yells as Andrews feints at her, tries to swing. He feels better than he has in months. Life is coursing through his body. It is as if he is back in conditioning, running laps, working the G-force simulator. He is aware of everything: Burns's sick pallor as he sits on the bed, Charlotte's tense crouch of fear and anger mingled with something else, her ragged breathing, the slight breeze that touches the sweat on his face and arms and moves the curtain from the pale light of the full moon into the bedside lamp's incandescence, his hands opening and closing as Burns waves Charlotte aside, looks at Andrews sadly, and asks, "Do you want to talk about it?"

Yes, there are climaxes, brief spurts of passion, jumps of energy, but they resolve nothing. The stories do not end neatly, much as we need them to. Our lives are incomprehensibly tangled. The need for climaxes and resolutions drives us to our madnesses, our fictions. For the world is round and nothing but round, there are only the soft risings and failings, the continual fall of day into night, the endless plummet through space without end or beginning. We drift, we live, we die, but death is not an end because the race goes on building pyramids and roads, launching rockets. Survive or perish, we each fill some role. But he is not a hero or a myth. Mere night rushes past his car. Three billion people on a single planet, the moon's dead light upon them.

He looks at the speedometer and sees with shock the needle at 100. He slows, the Thruway slows beneath him, and he drives calmly all the rest of the way back to Teaneck.

That week his book proposal is returned with a polite letter; his name at least has brought him the courtesy of a personal response. The editor explains how interesting the poetry looks, how intrigued he is by the prospects, but why he must reluctantly refuse. The letter goes on to state that an account of his voyage would be of interest, but he is no longer assured of selling even that on the strength of his name.

The next day he gets his renewal notice from the Air Force. He thinks of his $2,500 a month, he thinks of Kevin's college, he thinks of his $20,000 in the bank. He has two days to decide. He thinks of four years ahead of him, of retirement and pension at forty-four.

With Kevin, he watches the last Apollo unfold on television. They have been in orbit for two days now. NBC shows film of the launch. He hears Mission Control count down in its clear passionless voice. Andrews tenses, remembering the rocket's thrust, that great fist crushing him, solid ground falling from him, the horizon canting in the window, blue sky fading to black, the noise of the booster dwindling, gravity abating, and then the slow silent dance of Earth below. On the screen, smoke curls, cables fall, but the rocket is still, even past zero. In the cabin it feels like liftoff starts ten seconds early; from the ground it appears ten seconds late.

Now the rocket moves. The Saturn V has generated sufficient force, and it rises, slowly, majestically disencumbering itself of gravity. What sexual energy a rocket had. Charlotte had been at the lunar liftoff and she said later it was so sensual, so compelling, that warm sympathetic pulsings had started within her. When it was over, she said, people hurried away, awed and embarrassed by that immense potency.

Or, rather, force: for NASA had stripped rockets of potency. The first rockets delivered missiles. They flew, fell, exploded. Their trajectories were dramatic curves. But at science's imperative, now they flew straight up, out, dropped stages to hurl a payload of men at a weightless point in the sky. There was no arc to that, no climax. Andrews sees now that drama and sex are inextricably linked, that the rise and curve of one is the same as the other. Anything without a climax is ultimately disappointing. Give us missiles, not spaceships.

NBC is live again. The two ships orbit. The screen is dark with static and crackling voices. They are positioning a camera to follow the docking. The Earth rolls slowly beneath, Apollo roams the skies. Over the far curving horizon is a dot, a hint of movement. Soyuz approaches, gaining dimension. It elongates. There is a garble of static, Russian, and English mixed.

"Can you understand it, Dad?"

"Shh."

The Russian manned program will continue, he has heard. So, imagining himself in space, he feels vaguely threatened by the sight of Soyuz. Perhaps he projects his own tension into the voice of the American pilot, but he seems to Andrews as jauntily nervous as a virgin on his first date.

The far craft inclines in its approach. The two ships whisper through vast statics, they make minor adjustments as their trajectories close. The radio energy is dense as they make ready to touch. Electrons move, patterns shift. Data flickers in great networks around the world.

Kevin is leaning forward, his breath coming quick and shallow. In the moment before contact he hunches, feeling the shadow of contacts to come in this one. In the screen's light Andrews sees everything embedded in its moment: blue flickers on the wet brown beer bottle he has not touched, Kevin's rapt face washed pale, his own reclining posture, a roll of fat at his once-solid belly.

The ships link. Apollo mates with Soyuz. The gates are open, static floods between them, the astronauts and cosmonauts can move between vessels. The mission is consummated, the program is over. The camera drifts and Earth swims slowly under it. Ochres, blues, whites, haloed in static. The moon forgotten.

Something recedes in Andrews.

It is his fortieth birthday.

In the yard he studies the moon, and the empty blackness where the two vessels reel and clasp each other. The crews will shuttle between crafts for a bit, trade dull laborious jokes and dry paste meals, then disengage and return to Earth, nothing reached, nothing resolved. The first time America pulled back from a frontier.

When he goes in, Kevin is gone. He turns off the television. On impulse he goes to the attic to get the heavy binoculars he bought years ago in Okinawa. There is the smell of time behind the attic door, a musty wasting smell that makes him feel heartsick and lost. The attic is neat and orderly, but he cannot find the binoculars. Finally he steps back out, shuts the door.

He stands in the hall, feeling the house's emptiness. He listens to its hums and murmurs. Downstairs in the dark the refrigerator turns on. He is numb. He stands in a paralyzed panic at the top of the long dim stairway, unmoving for several minutes.

There is a ringing in his ears now and his hands are cold. He drifts down the hall into Kevin's room. It is dark, with only a pale illumination flooding from one window. The moon is gibbous again, waning back through all its phases. It is very late, after midnight; a new day has started.

Kevin lies angled back on the bed, binoculars propped by thin white arms bent double against his chest. Andrews enters but does not sit on the bed for fear of breaking the view. Nor does he speak. A minute drags by. Andrews is trembling. He says, "What do you see?"

His son shrugs. "Craters."

He looks and sees the blurred patches of gray against white. Copernicus, Ptolemy, Clavius . . . the dead. He feels remote and cold and untouchable. Kevin looks at him.

"Dad? Are we ever going back there?"

He sighed, tired, or on the edge of sorrow, though sorrow was a pointless thing. Waves receded from him. Each word broke a vast illimitable silence. "I don't know, son. I don't know."

A CATASTROPHE MACHINE

Strait is the gate, and narrow is the way, which leadeth into life,
and few there be that find it.

—MATTHEW 7:14

1.

I WAS twelve in the autumn of 1960, and my entrance into
puberty was not through sex, which I took more or less in
stride, but through the straiter gate of science. At this remove I
will not insist on the connection, but compare the two largest,
most optimistic American magazines of that time, the one of
sex and the one of science. More than once I hid the contents
of one within the covers of the other.

My world was based on analogy then. If the sun were an
orange, the earth was an appleseed ten yards on. If the earth
were a day old, man's history spanned five minutes. The sharp
shift of scale that these comparisons afforded pleased me. Metaphor lived for me with the authority of physical law. Some never
outgrow this state, and for some others the growth goes past the
bounds of life.

I worked square roots longhand for pleasure. I built models, of airplanes, autos, war machines, so carefully that I might have been confirming a paradigm of reality, and not just filling an idle afternoon. These at least are the memories I have of that time. There is no telling what distortions hindsight has worked on them.

In that large American magazine of science I read: "Elementary catastrophes may be generated at will with a simple device made of cardboard, rubber bands, and a few other materials." I was not surprised to read something so frivolous and unlikely about catastrophes. I still took my analogies on faith.

In the austere vocabulary of mathematics, a catastrophe is not just a sudden turn of violence. It is a set of conditions under which steady change may cause abrupt effects. At some point in a war of forces one gives way. A twig bends until it breaks. A seed withers or germinates. An unstable compound explodes. The earth quakes. And so on.

I understood none of this at first. I built the device from the pictures in the magazine. A cardboard disk turned smoothly to tighten a rubber band, which, at its extremity, abruptly snapped the disk back to its starting point. It was dull play. I worked it a few times, then put it away.

It might have remained in my cabinet until vanishing under my mother's statute of limitations on bizarre playthings, but one day I was ill and stayed home from school. After an hour of reading I was bored and thought of my catastrophe machine. I played with it for a while and formed a crude first idea of its simple workings.

When my father got home that night he slammed the door, cursed, and before greeting us poured himself a drink. He had almost run our Studebaker off the road. The brake line had ruptured, and he had swerved across two lanes of traffic to avoid hitting a truck. I made no connection.

The next Saturday morning I was killing some time before a

football game, sitting in bed with the machine propped on my stomach. When I left for the field I forgot all about it. Then, running for a pass, looking back over my shoulder, I slipped and struck my midriff hard across the goalpost. I lay without moving. I spent six days in the hospital with a ruptured liver; when I reentered the quiet of my room, and saw the machine still on my bed, I began to understand.

In high school I was shy and devoted myself to mathematics. The school was a blockhouse of what was called progressive learning, one of those flat sprawling monstrosities that flourished like mushrooms across the suburbs of the sixties. No community among the students, no language we shared, could resolve those blank lines of fluorescent tubes, the enameled expanse of lockers, the array of audiovisual aids, the rooms with sliding partitions, the diminishing prospects of the halls, into any personal meaning. Each faced this limbo on his own; each sought a particular significance. So the experience of the school was driven like an auger into the privatest recess of one's mind; the school offered itself to me in long, pointless dreams, but everything about it baffled explanation. It was preparing us for something, no doubt, something as elaborate and contingent as its own being, and if pressed about what that something might be, a teacher or a counselor might at last say "life." Anything but.

There was a computer. In those days this was rare. It was the pride of the math department: a teletype terminal connected by phone to a small machine at an RCA factory thirty miles away. Our school rented time along with fifty other schools and businesses. I learned the crude language of programming, its iterative logic, and started to work on a simple two-dimensional catastrophe program.

The formulae in my article were no longer obscure to me. With the computer I modeled my simple device and more intricate ones. By stages I came to understand catastrophes, their factors and generation. I drew curves on graph paper and built more elaborate devices from cardboard, rubber bands, the springs from ballpoint pens which my father manufactured, parts from an Erector set, small electric motors. The most elaborate of these machines I set up in my room, and let it run all day and all night; occasionally it would punctuate my sleep with the rasp of a spring releasing or a gear slipping from one position to the next, and in my dreams would come a fall.

In the back pages of that article the author applied his theory to a range of subjects: optics, seismology, embryology, propagation of nerve impulses, aggression, manic–depressive behavior, committee behavior, economic growth, national defense. The theory's value was this: it incorporated the qualities of discontinuity and divergence into models that could be used for prediction. In the biological and social sciences these qualities are often found, and account for the label "soft" or "inexact" sciences. Catastrophe theory, wrote the author, promised to be a major advance in making the inexact sciences more exact. What he meant was that the complexity of existence might be reduced to the paradigm of number.

Those mornings I rose early and read through the newspaper while my father shaved. The newspaper was also interested in catastrophes. I read: an atomic bomb was tested in the Nevada desert. A dam collapsed in Tennessee. An earthquake in California toppled houses. And so on. In these events I tried to find a pattern, a common ground of explanation in my theory of catastrophes.

About that time I found I could lay curses. They were effective in small matters such as games. I could cause ends to drop passes, and batters to swing at wild pitches, when I tried. I could make traffic lights turn. I told this to a friend, who scoffed, until on a hike he lost his footing crossing a stream, dropped a sandwich in the dirt, and spilled half a can of soda. Then the power became a grand joke between us, and we began attending sports in a spirit of scientific investigation and high delight at our secret. Perhaps neither of us believed it, or perhaps we did; for when at last the novelty of the delusion faded, and I declared that I would no longer use the power, the occasion turned solemn. I did not want to fool myself too much—just enough to enjoy a fantasy of control over a world in which, I knew even then, I was essentially powerless.

So I played at disasters. There was an ominous growth of pressure in the culture during these years, which I found modeled in a storm that gathered over our town in the spring of 1962, in clouds that I knew from my reading heralded a tornado. But this was New Jersey, where tornadoes were nearly unknown. The greenish light they cast made the town strange and fragile. My soul, too, felt strange and fragile as I watched the masses of air collide, their borders marked by shifting lines of gray, the most fearsome thing I had yet seen, and the air gusting now cold, now warm. A change of atmosphere made my ears ring. No funnels touched earth that day in New Jersey, not even a thunderstorm, but I felt the ground take in the energy of the thwarted storm. At night I felt the earth tremble more than from the passing trucks on the nearby turnpike.

My mother developed a disease. It was treated with radiation for a few months, but when its growth continued, her left breast was removed. Every week for a year she had radiotherapy. I came to look forward to Tuesday nights, when she and my father were gone over the bridge into the city for three hours. With the unforgiving absolutism of the young I saw the disease as weakness. And I saw weakness in my father's response: his depressions, his drinking. I separated myself from them in every way possible. Some evenings I ate alone in my room. At night I locked my bedroom door. Because they felt they had somehow failed me, because my mind intimidated them, they tolerated this, and solitude became my defense. Otherwise I might inherit their weakness.

I read: more complicated n-dimensional catastrophes may be

constructed by extending all the lower order catastrophes together with one new singularity at the origin. I adjusted my
machine accordingly. I watched the news.

Fires were set in South Boston. A helicopter crashed into a
crowd at a church picnic in Camp Hill, Pennsylvania. A new
strain of flu was detected in San Francisco. The United States
sent a few thousand military advisors to a country in Southeast
Asia. The Soviet Union installed missile bases in Cuba.

Probably I did not think that I was causing these events. I
was looking for a connection between myself and the world,
and my device was a metaphor. With it I cast myself into the
skein of cause and effect to see what I could learn. I built no
new machines, but created their mathematical equivalent as
computer programs. These became so complex that my teacher
wanted an explanation, but I was unable to find my article after
that, nor did I need it any longer. I just told him the work was
topology. He gave his permission to run an exceptionally elaborate program of loops, nests, chains, and subroutines. The date
was November 21, 1963.

We were all sent home early the next day. I was sick with
fever for a week. When I returned, the bill for my program
awaited me. I was almost expelled as a result, but a curious
technician at RCA had examined the program as it came over
the line, and the day after the bill came a job offer. So my escapade
earned me a reprimand and an A in math for the quarter.

But my behavior turned erratic, and I also earned some ses-
sions with the school psychologist, a sincere, plodding man, and
overweight. I did not tell him I felt responsible for the President's assassination; I did not dare! He has no sense of dread,
and I could tell he felt thwarted besides, so he would simplify
my own dread into neurosis.

Still, I sat in fear of the topic. I had such an elaborate and
lucid explanation of my role in the assassination that I could not

have kept from delivering a paranoiac masterwork had he once mentioned it. My program had gone out over phone lines, which linked the nation, which linked not just persons but machines, transmitters, who could know exactly what? The pattern of the program, which was catastrophic, might have influenced other patterns on the line, tipped them perhaps toward violence. Systems of social control were so complex and hidden, who could say which acts were trivial and which signified? So for the first time I was no longer playing. I had requested of some entity or some force a thoroughgoing catastrophe, and it had obliged me. Because of the mechanisms, because of the secret languages, my dark thoughts were no longer secret and personal. They had consequences.

The psychologist would have had a field day with my feverish theory. I sensed that my dread would pass, given time, but if he brought me to admit to it, I would be forced to defend it, and so might be locked into a widening system of delusion. So I kept counsel in the space of my mind, and fed him those, to me, harmless features of my home life he wanted to hear. I confessed guilt at masturbation, which I did not feel, and loneliness, which I did, and hatred of my parents, which he took at face value. His ultimate suggestion was that I try out for the baseball team that spring. And he said:

—You've a tremendous sense of responsibility.

To placate him and my parents, I did try out for the team. I remember the Saturday afternoons that early spring, narcotic as church, when my father coached me on pitching and batting stance in a bluff, raw voice. No player himself, his ignorance of the essentials was apparent even to me. His absurdity was mitigated only by his devotion; his earnest cries of encouragement smote the air like a distant parade. But my taste for sport was gone, as much from anguish over the idea of games as from my incompetence. My tryout was a disaster. After two weak hits I struck the ball soundly, and in utter astonishment watched as it fell past a chain link fence around left field. I promptly ran to third base. I suspect I did this on purpose.

That spring I fell in love. She was a Jewish girl a year older than me. My parents hated her, and hers me. Hers were survivors of a concentration camp, and my religion and ancestry were goads to their resentment, already large, for their daughter was a beauty, and she had talent, so she was bound to be separated from them. They had not yet accepted this. They tolerated me coldly. (My mother's response was more direct: she barred Lila from our house.) I was bright enough, I had manners, but I was a Gentile and, worse, a German. It was her idea to drive into the country for our own Seder and picnic on quiche Lorraine, but on our return, their furious faces, the dark mute clothes they had worn to temple awaited us on the porch, and their attitude said they saw me behind her every rebellion.

We pleased each other. I loved her will and her spirit. How unlikely I found it that she could love me. Once we were surprised when they came home early, and rushed downstairs to greet them in the neutral ground of the living room, only to realize we were wearing each other's pants. When I left an hour later, wearing my own, her mother gave me a secret smile. Her father was less civil; another evening I arrived on a motorcycle, in a black sweater and leather jacket, and he observed that I looked like Gestapo. But we were not as close as they feared.

—They're impossible, she told me, her eyes flashing. —Find one of your own, they say. And who are they supposed to be, my own?

I knew I was not one. She spent that summer on a kibbutz and had an affair with a major in the Israeli air force. And the next fall she went off for a week with a Russian poet come to speak at her college. This was too much. She had some special grace of the flesh that surpassed my own poor flailings. And I knew she would have shared it with me, but I was young, and my puritan nature still enforced a tyranny over joy that she could not accept. So we ended it. Again I retreated to mathematics.

At Yale I studied topology. My only friend, Shulman, would come through my room, singing, —Oh, Francis will topologize. If not, the seagulls will come and pull out his eyes.

Shulman had a dual major in theology and literature, and was writing a paper on James Joyce and the early Church fathers. He styled me the antimony of St. Francis, who, legend had it, talked to birds, all because I once told him I thought seagulls stupid and filthy. So he warped a refrain from Joyce to twit me as I sat like a lesser friar over my books, a Daedalus of the airless realm of math.

—Topologize, pull out his eyes.

He said also that I must work hard because mathematicians burn out early. I liked him for his banter, for his liking me without deference. So I never admitted to him that it was, in fact, a deep fear of mine.

—Topologize, pull out his eyes.

Obsessed I may have been. But my work was so clear to me then. The structure of the age was loss. All effort led us only to loss—loss of talent, youth, strength, courage, home. Life could be modeled on loss, or so it offered itself to me in my first days away from home, when I felt powerless before it, and only the dark task of understanding how we were separated from everything we loved was worth pursuing. I would build a mathematics of loss, and thus be freed.

2.

A mathematics of loss. What else was catastrophe theory? I went to consult the original article. Imagine my bitter surprise when I could not find it, not in any magazine or journal from 1959, or 1958, or 1960, or any other year. The million-card catalog held nothing on the subject. So I was thrown completely on my own resources. I would have to construct my theory out of my own work and life.

My mother died. I had sworn not to attend either of their funerals but, taken by surprise, I did go. The service was held on a bright spring day at the Church of the Atonement, the Reverend Mr Powers presiding. My father, Catholic, and my mother, Methodist, in dreary compromise, like comparison shoppers, had settled on the Episcopal faith for their marriage. And so the Reverend Mr Powers, who had presided at that ceremony as well, was called by way of last request out of retirement for this last compromise.

I had taken confirmation training from him. It was his pleasure to parse the word atone as "at one", which was good etymology but weak theology. It placed his doctrine closer to Mary Baker Eddy than to Richard Hooker; the sense of sin was small in his parish, and so, therefore, was the sense of responsibility. I had not been at one with the church since my confirmation.

At the service I was in good if nervous humor, and made dry jokes that passed unnoticed. My father seemed unmoved, and my mother's relatives shunned him. On our way home we stopped at a bar, and we drank together until sunset. He told me something I had already known: after the operation my mother had not let him touch her, and had then accused him of having affairs. For the first time he looked old to me.

—But it wasn't true. I never looked at another woman, all the time we were married. She seemed to want to destroy everything we had before the end. As if . . . she didn't want to owe me anything. The last thing she said to me was: I know you never loved me. Never! As if thirty-three years could count for nothing.

I stared out the window, clean of grief. I had not wanted to owe anything either.

—It was a relief, finally. I couldn't have taken it much longer. Do you . . . do you hate me?

His hands shook, and it struck me that despite all experience he was still a child. Married in the Depression, he had wanted to play trumpet in a band, she to sing. This they laid aside for love. He went to night school, she became a secretary. He found work in a watch factory. Young and innocent, they lived on New York's Lower East Side. He went to war, returned, and as if that had burned free a block in his genitals, they had at last their only child, myself. He bought a business in the suburbs. Friends moved west. They mortgaged a gracious home. Their lives crumbled inconspicuously. From the magic of those first years to pushing a cart in the broad aisles of the A&P, pushing an electric mower over tracts of sod, nothing in their youth— when marriages were forever, when cigarettes were social grace and not carriers of disease, when, if you lived under the roof of family, faith, and work, you were protected, and no calamity came unprovoked or undeserved—had prepared them for this world. Nothing accounted for this malaise. They could not understand what had failed; why they would leave the television on till three in the morning, its hum and flicker mediating dreams too bleak to face unsuccored; why faith had yielded to life insurance; why absences no longer promised return. But, young and bitter, I knew. I was older at twenty than he would ever grow. All their weakness was stamped on my soul as a lesson. I knew the secret was to cut free from anything that might lure you into sleep.

—No, I said obliquely. —I don't hate you.

I watched my father drink, and I wondered what greater distances would separate me from any children I might have.

After this I saw him seldom. On holidays he went to his brother's; I stayed in New Haven, working in my apartment, walking the slushcovered walks between the grotesque Gothic buildings, enjoying the peace of the empty campus. After this his drinking became serious. When he was committed to the sanatorium I refused to sign the papers, so my uncle, over no objections from me, obtained a power of attorney to do so. I met my uncle there, and he accused me of coldness. He described to me a person I had never seen in my father. Standing in the chill corridors of the clinic near Princeton, we might have been speaking of different men. He said my father cried each Christmas; he said he feared I had cut him off forever, that he worried constantly about my life, my happiness, my future. I was near to furious, for my father and I had spoken before of loneliness and the hardness of life, and if he had seemed at times naive, at least he had never fallen on the cheap sentiment my uncle claimed for him now. If he had known my father longer, still I knew him better; I allowed him his dignity, even when his mind was scattered from electroshock. It cost me to see him then. And I resented my uncle making a palimpsest of his brother's face, printing on it only those griefs and failures he suspected himself capable of—my proud uncle, a Vietnam veteran with two adopted Asian children of his own, and God knows what guilt—when I knew my father to be stubborn, independent, guiltless. He as much as said the drinking was all my fault, still asking me to sign.

—You're all he has left now. Help him.

Help him? I had seen cured alcoholics before. They were docile. Their cure was amputation. They did not face the cause or consequence of their drinking, except in execration. I would sooner see my father dead than bullied into that confession and self-censure. Let him choose his own fall. My uncle had to sign the papers.

In 1968 I submitted my master's thesis, "On Mathematical Modeling in the 'Soft' Sciences," and a week later received a job offer from a consulting firm.

The firm's name, NOUS (Nexus for Optimal Use of Science), was suggested by the Greek νους, meaning mind. Depending on the humor of the moment, it could also stand for Necromantic Oracle for Undermining the State, National Organization for Unemployed Scientists, New Oligarchs of the United States, or, miracle of brevity and arrogance, the French for *us*. They owned a building with a blank travertine facade in southern California, and flew me there for an interview.

Inside the noncommital shell of the building were a hundred modular offices. All walls were movable. System prevailed. The president spoke to me in a back room that overlooked the Pacific Ocean. He tapped my paper with a penpoint.

—We believe you're on the edge of some very interesting work here.

—That's obvious, I said curtly. I had made up my mind not to be impressed.

—Most of our work is advisory. We list options. We hope to guide our leaders to choices based on science rather than bias or ideology.

—Most of your work is military, I pointed out.

—We came into existence in 1963. We received a grant from the Ford Foundation. We received contracts from the Defense Department, which stipulated that only twenty percent of our research could be nonmilitary. Presently forty percent is. In five years it will all be.

He smiled and held up a single page.

—See this? This is a study done by the Hudson Institute, eighteen months' work; it boils down to this one sheet: a list of eleven probable directions for our society for the remainder of the century. It's worth a million dollars. We call this 'paper alchemy.' The entire annual output of our company could fit into a single volume. Now, this single sheet is worth a million dollars because of its credibility. Because certain people believe in Hudson's work. The bulk of Hudson's work is war-related. That establishes legitimacy. Then a study like this is taken seriously. We would like to be in such a position. We think it's important to establish legitimacy, by any means, because, frankly, eight of these eleven courses are not desirable. And without adequate counsel, the government may very well adopt the wrong course.

—May I see that?

—It's classified. He put the paper away. —We can offer you twenty thousand a year and absolute freedom. Work on what you like. Our facilities are better than any university's, and your time will be your own.

—My own? In what sense?

—In whatever sense you care to take it. We don't employ people. We offer fellowships. A sense of community.

As I considered this, he turned from me to watch the ocean breaking on the shore below.

I returned east and spoke to Shulman. His work now was advising conscientious objectors in a small office on campus. When I said I might join NOUS, he said, —That's like Joyce writing brochures for the Catholic Aid Society.

—Do you despise them so much?

—Francis, do you know who these people are? These people brought you the Gulf of Tonkin. They practically sponsored the Bay of Pigs. Lyndon goes on TV seated at a desk because there's a NOUS employee under it sucking him off.

—I don't think they like the government.

—No, of course not, they feel themselves superior to it.

—Well, so do you.

—Oh, a true thrust. Two points for that. The difference is that I know how powerless I really am, and these people act as if they're inspired by God, no, worse, by science, and so can disavow responsibility for their acts.

—They don't act. They list options.

—Ironic that you of all people should be attracted by this austere bullshit amorality. Or is it? I suppose it was in you all along, the cunning in your silence.

—Are you speaking as a friend, I asked with heat, —or as a Jew studying under a Jesuit?

He stared bleakly out the window.

—Laurence. I want a place to work. Mathematicians burn out early, you know.

—A home, he said and turned back to me. —Then for heaven's sake, find one, make one, but not there.

—Their war work establishes legitimacy.

—The legitimacy of war, perhaps. Would you fight in this one?

—No. But if I turn them down I may have to.

—There are teaching posts at McGill, he said, reaching for a catalog.

—No, I said. I spoke carefully now, more afraid of lying to myself than to him. —I won't run. I must understand this. It frightens me, but I can't ignore it. Last year, when you wanted me to march, I wouldn't, and it was this same fear, this fear of avoidance. I avoid real commitment. And I'm afraid avoidance will destroy me. But that was what I saw at your meetings, in the best and worst of your people, the dropouts and the Marxists with private incomes; I saw this avoidance, everything I hate in myself. They were committing to nothing but a style or a program, and so refusing to commit personally, to avoid complexity or complicity, do you see? You said yourself they'd rather be getting high.

Again he looked outside. —The time I spend in here, arguing with assholes, deadbeats, chickenshits. All worried about their own asses. You're right, of course. But I tell myself it's good to deprive the Army of any warm bodies. And now I have to watch a genuine mind bought out by these fuckers? I'd rather be getting high myself. Christ, Francis.

—I do math, and I'm vain enough to think I can do original work. I won't spend my best five years grading papers. Tell me I'm rationalizing. But it will take all my courage to do this.

—Chessmen, he said.

—A cheap metaphor, Laurence.

There was a stale silence in the office. At last he sighed.

—Take the job. Do your work. Don't let them bind you. The mind, you know, is fallible.

After his cure my father took an apartment near his brother's house. Our house was sold. Before leaving for California, I went home to clean out my room. Carefully I crushed my models and sorted books. All tokens of my younger self I rejected, except the most elaborate of my catastrophe machines. It looked like a toy; too, it was a symbol. It marked a line dividing play from the stern art of the real. Even so, I did not work the device. I still feared it. I took it with me.

I was welcomed to Los Angeles by the shooting of Robert Kennedy. An auspicious sign, since I had done nothing, I thought, to provoke it. I was twenty-two, the youngest man in the firm; and they were all men, the NOUS fellows. The only women were secretaries.

Shulman was right. The rule at NOUS was legitimation without God. There was the attitude that we were the episcopacy of the mind, the cryptarchs of the state. We were a meritocracy, the elect, unimpressed by the government or the governed, and aloof from both the presbyters and the preterite.

Our real work, I came to see, was legitimation. Once power is acquired it must be kept. Armies of lawyers, writers, and priests are employed to shape the language to serve the ends of that power. The ultimate legitimation is the appeal to God. Protestant America, having delegitimated the Pope and royalty, needed a new ultimate that was neither the will of the people nor the authority of the individual soul. It was science. And mathematics was in its service. Technicians were its priests, and NOUS its bishopric.

Here I watched everything through the lens of catastrophe. War was a conflict of forces ending with victory and loss. The earth moved in response to equations of catastrophe. Alcoholism was catastrophe: one drank continually, until one could not stop. Learning was catastrophe: one studied till one day the knowledge was owned. History itself was a downward gyre, its line marked by events, the horizontal thrust all good intentions, the vertical drop the gravity of our situation. And so on. These were the idle-hour thoughts I indulged in my cube of an office, overlooking the new priesthood at play in the courtyard swimming pool. My work went well at first, but I felt engulfed. Nothing I could do placed me outside the mathematics of catastrophe. No move was free. Each devolved through the landscape of its cusps and curves.

We were in fact the model citizens of our own minds. The closed environment was exemplified by the game rooms, in which endless reflection and calculation and refinement were possible without critique; they were a perfect escape from the ungovernable complexities of the real into that simpler world of artifact that had nurtured all our narrow talents from the start. In the game rooms futures were built and wars played out, and not just the current war in Southeast Asia; they foresaw others. Favorites were an American civil war in 1985, a Mideast oil war in any year with varying protagonists, a limited nuclear war in Sweden in 1990, or, the favorite, a test of nuclear deterrence that invariably ended in planetary destruction. NOUS modeled even themselves, in a game designed to improve the modeling process at NOUS.

But they played ultimately for the sake of play. Every act was revocable, every move but a tentative step toward a changeable model of the narrowest gate into the real. Every bad idea, every mistake, could be shredded or revised in some new context. These fellows were the ones I had seen in the Yale computing center after midnight playing "space war," the ones who would yet bring on a real war in space.

One night the blank travertine facade was painted with a red hangman's knot. The president's comment was: —I'd give that a seven for wit, and a two for taste. Some credited the hostility to the accident of the word *game*. Popular opinion said that games about Armageddon could be played only by frivolous ghouls. Within NOUS a game meant only a situation where interests conflicted. It was a question of language. But I would maintain that in language there are no accidents. The word showed sharply a confluence of thought particular to our work and attitudes.

In short we were creators of fictions, and worked ultimately for our own satisfaction. So, although I did not work on the reports, the twenty-page skyblue folders marked secret that might sell for fifty or a hundred thousand dollars, I felt . . . what? I felt nothing. NOUS was not home, I kept telling myself. In the first month I modeled the differentiation of tissues in an embryo and the epidemiology of a flu strain. I passed up my chance at nuclear wargaming, though a couple of fellows dropped by my office to hint at how well my work might fit with theirs. Not home, but a sort of refuge.

In a kind of concession to my new station I went home for the holidays the next two years, to my uncle's house. Each year I greeted my father, settled into the guest room (my father stayed in Decha's room, who slept with his sister for the week); I walked with my father in the mornings, when he was not so bad, played touch football with the kids for a banal and irritating week. My relatives, arrived for drinks, would talk about my father in the third person, though he was in the room. I irritated my uncle in turn with tales of my work.

—I'm only a chicken colonel, he would respond, his Georgia voice rich with the ironies of his success, he, who had quit high school to fight in the Pacific, who climbed the ranks in combat, in three wars, while I, educated, intelligent, pretended involvement at the edge, —but I don't see why they waste money on a bunch of pardon my French goddamned theorists. We could clean that place out in a year if they let us. Charlie runs into Cambodia and we stand there wavin' good-bye. The safest place to stand in a mortar attack is next to the Shell Oil truck. Nobody there knows spit from Spinoza.

Expressions like these were to prick my intellectual vanity, as he saw it.

—Would you go back? I asked.

—No thank you. No sir. It's no war. We should pull the hell out before we lose everything.

—There we agree.

—Is that how you advise the Pentagon? he laughed. —They must like that.

—We don't advise. We list options.

—Why don't you go if you know so much?

—The DOD finds my work here more valuable.

What it cost me to say so. To shut him up I had let out my dread. My true work was so obscure that I doubted its use to anyone, but NOUS had no such doubts. For they were engaged in the large sterile work of legitimating themselves. That was the code in which all their reports were written. And their work's ultimate meaning was only what it revealed to them about the nature of their own intellects. Whereas I was sure only that nothing could be truly known, because the very act of knowing involved a radical doubt that must question even itself.

As time passed, the less adequate my mathematical haven seemed. I missed the evidence of the senses, the tangible persuasions of impure reason. I needed an arena in which I could act bravely and well. Again a sense of sex awakened in me. Again I fell in love. I married Alice.

We were each young and unhappy, and so our life together was at first a succession of gifts. Her first husband had been my opposite: a pragmatic engineer, outgoing, respected, adjusted, and a model of consideration. Except in bed. There his special pleasure was ferociously to bite her breasts and thighs. He claimed she enjoyed it. She thought it was his way of leaving secret marks upon her that no other could see. So I was careful to handle her like satin. And she did nothing to startle my pleasure, to scare it from deepening into real feeling, as it seldom had in my poor five years of love. We named our acts. Our love talk was words neither of us had used with other lovers, and even our mundane household conversations were clipped, incantatory, definite, and kept alive our appetites. We fucked long hours, in a hundred ways, fast, slow, desperately, minimally, in the depths of feeling and the shallows of pleasure, as if seeking some point past that of release, as if to trick or drive the orgasm into a confirmation. This could not last. After all, we were using each other to prove our authenticity, to identify self to self, and in the end nothing is more dispiriting than using sex to keep track of one's psyche, nothing so disheartening as seeing the clock in the eyes of your lover.

Empiricists make the worst romantics. It was bound to end. Later I gave reason after reason on the analyst's couch and in talks with a few friends, and none of them were true. It may be usual to miss the reasons and retain only certain pictures. Here is one picture. Alice was prone to bad dreams, and had been since youth. And I could not bear to be touched in my sleep. So whenever I heard her start to toss and groan, I slid to the far edge of the bed and buried myself in a feigned sleep deeper than true. If her dreams were very bad, the old bed would quiver and cast me like a beached fish onto insomnia's shore. But one night in my sleep I heard her cry, and I turned at once to comfort her. I held her desperately, as if she might in an instant slip into the dream and away from me forever. And at that moment a small dry voice spoke to me with the absolute authority of sleep. It said: —Now you are truly lost. My grip awakened her. We made love, and afterward she slept, but I was turned from sleep the rest of the night.

She became pregnant. She wanted the child and I did not. Childhood was the greatest of indignities, a prolonged insult, and I could not wish it upon another. I insisted on abortion, and she refused. I swore if she had the child I would put it up for adoption. If it came to that, she yelled, she would leave me and raise it herself.

And she left me, taking the child, the boy. Not for two years did I realize that I had wanted the child even more desperately than she. That I had needed her to fight me, not to flee, to deliver me of my true feelings. But I was unable to provoke her into the violence necessary to show me what I had to learn. How could I have known that my belief in marriage would prove so large? We had almost omitted the ceremony. And not till after this did I realize the depth of Shulman's perception in his office when he had said: a home. That was indeed what my willful, juvenile psyche had seen in NOUS—the first evidence in my life of love for the wretched thing I had made of myself, not for what I could be or had been given. And that was what Alice and the boy had been, too: a way back to a home I had lost. Shulman sent me a postcard in those days that read in part, *wise poet Williams sings, "divorce is the sign of knowledge in our times, divorce, divorce!"* and still I did not understand. The hard navigator of my soul commented in its unhelpful taciturn style, *loss frees*, but I knew that to lose something not yet understood binds one helplessly to the understanding of it.

So the cold home of math opened itself to me again. I began to smoke, I used a year's leave in a month, I became jealous of my work, separating what I did for NOUS from what I did for myself, though they had a legal right, I learned as I read my contract for the first time, to anything I put on paper. I did less and less for them. In an access of ambition, as if my mind mocked my heart in its freedom and sought an immense project to immensely bind it, I planned a book on the history of thought—no less for this lessened soul!—followed in mathematics. I began to trace the, to

me, true histories of certain ideas: the discrete and the continuous, the transinfinite and the imaginary. I felt that I was uncov-
ering the broken spires of some vast architecture of thought, and
in time could excavate a buried city of intellect. It might take me
twenty years.

I did not force it: I wrote perhaps a page a day, but they were
firm; each day I went back and made tentative connections
clearer. Statements fell definite and concise as the edges of a
polyhedron. My title was *Noetics*.

But in the meantime I was bound daily to catastrophe theory.
NOUS now wanted a book on it. The discipline was mine; no
one else had thought to apply discontinuous topologies to modeling, and they were anxious for applications. So I struck a deal.
For fifteen thousand in advance I would give them a book in a
year, and I would work at home.

Day to day I slept late, breakfasted on orange juice and coffee,
walked to the beach and back, read the paper, watered plants,
sat at my desk, smoked, went to the library, sat in a park, came
home, poured a drink, then another, and no work came. Some
mornings I awoke resolved to break my habits, no cigarettes,
no coffee, no drinking, and by evening I was again drunk and
desperate in a smoky room. I would sit dull and dazed before
the dead glass eye of the television and try to lose myself in the
atrocious films of the war, the banality of the comedies, the
assault of ads, all wit, courage, and technique compressed into
the flat travesty of that awful screen, and still my mind ground
on, still I tried to find a thread of connection between what I
needed from life and what was offered to me here.

For months I bullied myself through night after fruitless night.
I dozed over my papers. Once I dreamed the finished book on
my library shelf. They were bound in black cloth. I could read
neither the title nor my name on the spine. I took it down and
opened it. The pages were coarse black paper, ragged at the

edges. The text was obscure and illegible. I turned the pages with mounting anxiety. I could just make out where the text broke for the formulae and illustrations, but nothing was readable.

Then my block broke, and I wrote for five full days, excited and confident. I even added pages to *Noetics*, so cleanly were my thoughts breaking between the mathematics NOUS wanted and the philosophical inference I was saving for myself. The bones of all my future work were there. Now I might quit NOUS, I was free, for I had seen at last that loss was simply a component of growth, and that my work was therefore leading surely into biology, into life, into some grace of unity. I nearly wept with delight and self-love as I found my way fully into the modeling of embryology, cell motility, mitosis. At last I was content. I took a rest.

In the morning mail was the new *Topology*, and on page 313 began a long article titled "Topological Models in Biology." I began to read. I skimmed. I turned pages furiously and finally pushed the journal aside. I knew it all. It was my book.

I was humiliated. All the months of sweat, the fear that I might never work again, the flesh of my life I had fed my theory, were pointless, because the work had been done anyway. It had been taken from me before its term.

I looked for my master's thesis, to compare it, to establish for my sanity's sake my priority, but I could not find my copy. I called Yale. And I learned that NOUS now held the only copies; they had pulled Yale's, invoking security. So I drove to NOUS, and I remember the brown pall over the city, but whether it was from brushfires, or pollution, or a ghetto burning that day, I in my hermitage and obsession could not say, and when I parked in the seaside lot, the smoke was no longer visible.

A new device had replaced the security guard; fumbling, I fed it my pass, and the outer door clicked to admit me. Within

I spoke to a secretary I had not met before; she resembled Alice.

—I'd like to access Eckart's paper on modeling, I said, using their idiom.

She looked it up and asked if I had clearance.

—I'm Eckart, I said, smiling. I held out my pass, thumb covering as if by chance the clearance number next to my name and photo. She would not, I thought, question the author. Chances were my clearance was legitimate anyway. But I felt like a thief.

She smiled and handed me keys. —Here you are. Room thirteen, drawer thirty.

I had some trouble finding room thirteen. The door numbers were out of sequence. The halls now seemed to spiral inward. I passed and repassed a lounge, recognizing two men there, the sea curling slow as a yawn beyond them. They did not see me. I could not recall their names.

Finally I found it: two black adhesive numerals slightly askew on a fireproof door. Drawer thirty was midway down the second row, also labeled: DOD-SBC-8-68-A. I unlocked it, rolled it open. It was stuffed with skyblue folders and a few red ones. In a blue folder I found my paper. There was an eight-page précis headed: "Option: Catastrophic Collapse of RVN Government, Tactics of Civilian Casualties." Appended to this, virtually as a footnote, was my work, fifty pages of photocopies.

I went to the president's office. His door was ajar. He was regarding the shimmering crawl of the ocean through his broad, tinted window.

—What is this? I said, extending the folder.

He turned in alarm. It took him a moment to recognize me. —That's classified. You haven't got clearance . . .

—It's my paper, for the love of Christ! I want to know why I found it with this.

—I'd like to know that too. He was composed now. He lifted

his telephone. —Peake? Have a look at room thirteen, there's been an unauthorized entry.

I shook the folder as he cradled the phone. —Don't you understand that this is mathematics? Pure?

—Everything pure gets applied, Francis. We deal in the art of the real.

—You, you want to outsmart the present, to think your way outside history. You, your games and models all come from a horror of time and the fear of change, because over time power can only dissipate itself. What you deal in is the opposite of the real.

He merely looked at me.

—You lied to me. You broke into my house, you stole my private papers. This, and this, and this. "History of the Transfinite," this is mine!

—You have no private papers. Our contract . . .

—Not this! Nothing gives you rights to this!

—You are courting serious trouble here, Francis.

—How did you get these papers?

—You might have sent those by messenger. We could produce receipts with your signature. Why, we could put you in jail. Not a hundred people in the country are allowed to see that folder.

I fumbled with my briefcase, spilling papers. I brought out the new *Topology* and threw it down. —Here. Read it, you son of a bitch. Then tell me what good this has done you.

Then I went to retrieve some books from my office. But the new arrangement confused me. Walls had moved. I found a men's room I remembered and backtracked from there. Where my office had been was now a lounge, overlooking the swimming pool. A couple of men smoking glanced at me without interest. As I stood another man came up behind me: Peake.

—You'll have to leave, Francis. You no longer have clearance to be in the building.

I was too angry to answer. I handed him my pass and turned to go.

—Please leave your briefcase. You can pick it up tomorrow after we've inspected it.

—Fine. Help yourself to my lunch.

Peake shook his head calmly. —Honestly, Francis. Did you think we kept you around for your looks? Your conversation?

—I thought I was here to do math.

—You were here to serve us. And now we are through with you.

Was it news to me that I had been an instrument? Confirmation, rather. I waited for dreams, for contrition, but my psyche was unwilling to penetrate the surface of the television's nightly war. No, my sleep was as placid as my sin was small. Its consequence was less than that of the least Wehrmacht bureaucrat okaying a boxcar of potatoes. Guilt? None, though my ego longed for it. I had been living the life of another. So my dreams brought no burning bodies to torture me, only dark, instantly forgotten images of abasement that tried to follow me up out of deep sleep and failed.

The one dream I recalled was of the engineers, the technicians, the cyberneticists, the two whose names I could not recall. They surrendered their bodies at a chrome altar, they joined the rest, linked englobed immortal brains they were, murmuring in binary tongue, wishing only for the last separation, the divorce from matter, the dialectic of phenomenon and noumenon conquered at last. I despised them. Yet, I was one of them, one who sought to leave his special marks where no other could see them. I was one who sought ultimate separation. And then, overriding the legitimations of sleep, came contrition, all at once; it came as my dream was bathed in impossible light, and even the shadows were sieved by radiance and my heart pierced with anguish, for here it was, the one conflict, the one war, the one separation we all truly desired, the one weapon that could

abolish matter, leaving no remnants, no evidence, the one logical outcome to all our labor, all our misdirected lusts, all our
will to loss. Dreaming, my mind was as a child's; and I remembered once burning a sex magazine in an access of shame, not
guilt, at masturbation; and now the Puritan in me decried my
small sin at NOUS as the pollution of all life, and cried for
another fire, for an eradication more thorough than that of
Sodom; so in my dream I called a bomb to Los Angeles, the
bomb that my forebears at a forerunner of NOUS had created;
and as it irrupted into my prior dream, I saw the worst, that I
had wanted this, that all dreams, even the most atrocious, are
truly wish fulfillments. And could I doubt that the shape of my
waking thoughts was congruent to my dreams? No. In the
mind's code my theory of catastrophes asked for just such an-
nihilations. So ideally I was responsible for any atrocity committed in the name of pure knowledge, just as I was guiltless of
any particular crime. That paradox, which I could not master
with words, would continue to deny me absolution.

Lacking words, I gestured. As a final gesture to childhood I
set the last and most complex of my catastrophe machines in a
crawlspace in my apartment. I sealed it in there, running on
long-lived batteries, and I left the apartment for good, taking
what books and clothes would fit in my car, and I checked into
a motel, a zone of spiritual parsimony and anonymity, as if chal-
lenging some power to bring me the worst. All I had made was
for play after all, the vacuous play of the self-intent. Nothing I
now did or could do would promote or impede the progress of
the immense catastrophe machine that was our culture.

After a time I called Shulman. He was gentle. He knew
someone at the university in Hume, and if I liked he would
mention my name. In two weeks it was settled. I had an asso-
ciate professorship at half my NOUS salary. I was twenty-five
years old.

3.

When I came to Hume I began to think I had been ill for some time. On my walks to the school I became appalled at the diversity of life the landscape offered. In a courtyard a cactus garden held a hundred species. Gold and black carp lazed in ponds. Eucalypti, redwoods, acacias, broke the air. The bougainvilleas, the fuchsias, flouted their sex. Even the twisted succulents in late spring sent up a tall twig crowned with tight rosy buds.

I was done with all this. The sexual transactions of my being proceeded on a level deeper than I cared to go. Surfaces tyrannized my attention. Listening intently, I found no moment free of sounds. Gazing at stars, I imagined their slow streaming, the eon-long flattening of constellations. Objects were lurid to my sight, and slipping across the edge of one to the next it suffered shock and dislocation. My body was a burden. Even the fog, once a balm, became hideous to me one night as I perceived its million particles swirling chaotically past my porch light. Each moment was booming agony, and had always been.

My students were near my age, alien otherwise. The sharp catastrophic cusp the culture had just passed—when exactly in my cloistered time had it happened?—had left an insuperable chasm. I guessed that some of them envied me and others despised me, but all we ever talked about was math. Last year students had been killed; the game of radical praxis had turned serious; terror was in the air; there had come a chill as final as the abrupt lock of water molecules at freezing. Some of these students kept up the forms of protest; but they were already looking for another, safer game.

In my free hours I watched the sea. It was great enough to swamp my senses. I would take a bottle of wine and pick my way down the steep hills seaside of the road and sit on some narrow stone ledge a few hundred feet above the water. I would drink wine and try to think of nothing. Often there was fog, and ideally I could see nothing but ten feet of rock face on either side of me. There I would sit until the chill came with the evening. The trick was to walk back drunk. I collected rocks on these outings, sandstone, basalt, serpentine, jade, and carried them in my windbreaker pockets for ballast. They swayed as I walked, pulling first one way, then another. Let it come. Let the last catastrophe take me, split the world, let the flowers and leaves blacken at their edges, curl, burn, let the fish bloat and poach in their ponds, the birds blaze like thrown firebrands, the rocks flow steaming to the sea, let the final decompression of matter come, and resolve all to all. A dozen times I saw it poised. The edges shimmered, but did not burn.

I sold my car. I had a dread of flying. Twice I was invited east, twice I made reservations, and twice I stayed at home, sitting in a cold sweat on my packed bags until the hour to leave had passed. I could feel clearly the plummet of the plane and the termination impending death would offer, the pattern of my life suddenly complete and irrefutable. Gravity would claim me; my situation at last clear, I would see just how badly I had lived, the constellation of each mistake, as I fell with strangers in a device not of my making.

My father called. His voice was hesitant. He asked if he might spend Christmas with me. I remembered other Christmases, the sad comedy of regrets and recriminations stored all year and brought out for display then because it was the one time of the year in our family when genuine feeling was called on: I, acting the part of the young scholar pleased with his annual respite, and grateful for the simple bourgeois conventions of turkey, liquor, ennui; my father so drunk he could hardly stand, but acting judicious and reserved; my uncle's bright brutal eyes clocking the room for the least evidence of ill will to transfix like a bug on the sharp point of his displeasure. The stupidest time of the year. Yet now I wanted him to come. I too had failed. I imagined him alone in his apartment, his drowned eyes, his limp hands, and thought, death is separation enough, no need to seek more. Yes, do come, I said in a voice no longer able to carry warmth. He said he would rent a car at the airport, and I recited slowly the directions to my house. He had me repeat them, then he read them back to me.

When he came we embraced. I had already had two drinks. He admired the house. I said I would take him to dinner. He fussed over the menu, said he could not eat this or that, asked the waiter how much salt was in each dish. He turned his empty wineglass upside down on the table. As we ate I spoke about my book and the university. In grief and shame I started to explain why I had quit NOUS, when he interrupted me.

—I'm proud of you, Fran. All you've done.

I could have cried. His piety sickened me. Was my life to vindicate his? How could I now explain to him my humiliation? Then I saw. With bright wounded eyes he still sought forgiveness for that which needed no forgiving. The giving up of his vice had stripped him of all dignity. He moved and spoke slowly and cautiously. Every gesture betrayed a man who had been whipped to within an inch of his life and now distrusted his every instinct. So he had nothing left to rely on but the empty forms of manners, platitudes, and that failure of feeling called sentiment. There was no strength in him, and I was ashamed that I had looked for any.

Through this I bolted two glasses of wine. He leaned over and tapped my wrist, saying:

—You know . . . you ought to be careful. These things may be in the blood, they say. You know. Hereditary.

I looked away, sure I would be sick. Some transaction of spirit occured in my stomach, and I did not resist it. I swallowed my nausea, then lit a cigarette, as if to bring it back. I was sure he would say: *that too.* But he was more oblique.

—Your mother, for all her faults, was a fine woman.

Could he not let me be? Would he force on me a fall not my own?

—Oh yes, a fine woman. Who made life hell for us both. Do you remember when she told Lila she wouldn't have yids in her house? Or when she called the police the night you slept in the guest room, told them you had a whore with you?

—She was sick. The poor woman was on drugs, getting ready to die. You know that.

—I won't argue. It's past. If you want to forget it, fine. But it's obvious what you went through. What we both went through.

—Don't speak ill of the dead.

He meant himself. So he was dead to me, and I to him. All at once I needed to see Alice. I needed to explain what had gone wrong between us, why she could love and I could not. I wanted to see my son, now three years old, and warn him against the world he would have to enter. I wanted to know his first word. But I no longer knew where they lived. Like my father, I was past reclamation, and against my will was forced to this knowledge: nothing can be reclaimed, for we have no claims to faith, love, loyalty, or anything we touch, besides those we establish furtively and spend our spirits legitimating. This surge of feeling, like a flower unfolding, like first sex, like the bloom of bombs over a distant jungle, wrung from me the last tear I would ever shed in sorrow.

My father saw it and clutched my hand. Shivering with shame and revulsion, forcing myself to forget that there was nothing in him to which I could speak, surrendering at last, I pressed his hand in my own.

4.

Now I am older. I am dying of the worst of illnesses. The doctors say it is no worse than any other, but how can I believe that, when they are so helpless before it, so ignorant of its cause, and when its nature is so consonant with my own? I can find all the letters of its name among those of mine, and its name is the name of my birth sign. It is a disease of growth, but the difference between it and normal growth is so complete, and so subtle, that I believe it found its proper soil in my cells, the monads of my self—this disease of our time, whose manifold triggers lie in our landscape like some equation of consequence. It is my mother's disease. I tell them they could do worse than seek its cause in the theory of catastrophes.

I try to tell myself that there is no connection between the shape of my life and the shape of my end. But my heart does not believe it. And at this point, finally, in atonement, it is the heart I must trust.

Since I am dying they listen to me with tolerance, but for them my words already belong with the words of the dead. I have abandoned the cold comforts of topology and read now medieval and mystical texts—Ptolemy's *Almagest*, Swedenborg's *Arcana Coelestia*, treatises on astrology, numerology, demonology—the broken and unlegitimated paradigms of an earlier world, which seem, even in my removed state, less signposts in the history of ideas than the tortured, self-inflicted symbols of a deep, long, racial insanity, stages in the progression of a disease whose course has almost run to its conclusion.

My own work, *Noetics*, lies in ruins, a hundred disparate fragments of a few pages each, each a node of some intricate mapping of self that never revealed itself whole. How had I ever thought to do it? They are sunk like stones in my mind's mire. Each day I haul forth another, burn a few pages more. In my new, almost sensual appreciation of superstition, it would not surprise me to learn that each idea marked a like stage in the advance of my own disease, and the catastrophic surface they define is nothing but my own face. I understand at last that this is the life I designed for myself.

I thought my machine caused catastrophes. But I had no idea of their true nature: not quick, but lingering; not isolate, but consequential. Each linked to the next in an endless chain called life, beginning with the catastrophe of orgasm, the differentiation of tissues in amnion, the cord severed at birth. So we proceed by catenations of divorce, loss, and disease to the reward of death. I found life too painful to touch; by seeking the skeleton of catastrophe in every event, I was able to mock the bones of loss. Flesh now takes its due. And the whole culture binds itself to this new faith of loss, this new disease.

My father sends the latest journals. My theory is passing into public domain. It is finding applications. This month in the large American magazine of science is an article called "A Catastrophe Machine". There, at last, is the drawing from which I built my first simple device so long ago. How can I know what I am responsible for?

Probably my father will outlive me.

These last few weeks the pain has grown worse. My doctor offers me narcotics. So far I have refused.

BLUMFELD, AN ELDERLY BACHELOR

BLUMFELD, AN elderly bachelor, arrived home from work each weekday at six. From the highway he drove up a hill, where he could look back down on the traffic and congratulate himself on living where he did. A mere hundred yards past his offramp, traffic thickened and slowed where the highway narrowed to enter a tunnel through the hills into the further suburbs. By the time those cars arrived home, Blumfeld would be having his one drink of the evening, scanning his newspaper, and starting dinner.

Blumfeld's building was set back a slight distance from the highway. It was twelve stories tall and contained about five hundred apartments. Inside, all was of a comforting sameness. The corridors were identical and labyrinthine. Blumfeld lived on the eighth floor, but if the elevator happened to stop on seven, as it sometimes did, he might get off unaware, then smile and shake his head at the error.

Blumfeld's apartment was modern, with every convenience. It lacked nothing a reasonable man could ask. Three large chairs, a sofa with a foldaway bed, and a low glass coffee table dominated the living room. The kitchen alcove boasted a wood veneer table, a microwave oven, a garbage disposal in the sink, and a recessed motor near the stove that drove a generous variety of appliances. Of these Blumfeld used only the can opener. The bedroom was satisfactory; the bathroom had a heat lamp. The living room window overlooked the highway and the hill beyond. Blumfeld had lived here a year with no regrets. Monthly when the rent was due, he was a little surprised at the expense, but he was more surprised at how much of his paycheck remained. For Blumfeld was a man of modest wants and temperate habits, and his job as an accountant for a clothing firm in the city paid well.

He ate, saw that it had grown dark, and rose to turn on more lights, first pausing at the window. The traffic was again moving swiftly. He watched the streaks of red and white, and listened to the highway's muffled drone. Lights came on in a house on the hill beyond the highway. The figures of a man and a woman moved inside; they vanished from one window, and reappeared in another. He watched them with the placid interest of a well-mannered child. The lights went off, and a minute later they came on again in an upstairs room. The two figures appeared there. They embraced and kissed. They undressed, and Blumfeld saw the woman kneel at the man's feet. Abruptly, furiously, he pulled the curtain shut and turned on his lights.

Blumfeld considered his anger. He was a bachelor by choice, and considered his choice wise. The pleasure of sex in no way compensated his attendant loss of peace. But now he ran a hand through his thinning hair and felt a kind of loneliness. He would never have a woman kneel naked at his feet. It was not regret he felt, but passion. Yes, definitely, he was aroused—he, Blumfeld, whose sex life was normally confined to his dreams. He flung himself on the sofa, disconsolate. Angrily he loosened his trousers. He snuggled against a crevice in the cushions. He pressed his lips to the pillow by his head.

After a long while he got up drowsily. He undressed, put on

his pajamas, and turned off the lights. Contrary to his custom, he did not sit up in bed to read and smoke his single cigarette, but fell asleep at once, as if he has been purged of all habit.

Next morning Blumfeld was abashed. He had an impulse to beg forgiveness of his sofa, to address it as he had seldom spoken to a human being.

—I am losing my mind, said Blumfeld, but as he spoke he knew this was untrue. He felt rather that he was discovering his nature for the first time, and, appalled, he felt that it pleased him. I shall be someone after all, he thought.

In the office Blumfeld spoke sharply to his assistant. She had, for most of a month, entered a certain expense in the wrong column of the ledger. His words were in fact mild, but she was a quiet and sensitive woman and Blumfeld had never before criticized her. He had in fact, over the years, repeatedly spared her feelings, as it seemed to him now, at some expense to his own. Now, as Blumfeld spoke, she raised her hand to her mouth more from shock than pain. She ran from the office. Blumfeld felt that together they had celebrated some passage, and her eyes had moistened with tears of joy. For a moment he felt both fulfilled and desolate.

Driving home he was so distracted that he missed his exit. The apartment building, his home, dwindled behind him as he was carried forward against his will through the narrow tunnel, to the other end, where he crossed lanes of hostile drivers, exited, and returned. He was an hour late getting home. He was so distracted he could not eat, but flung himself on the sofa. He had practically forgotten the incident of the night before, but now, just inches from his face, was the zipper of a slipcover, partly open. As he touched it his hands trembled. He slid it open, speaking nonsense in a tender, cajoling voice. He undid his trousers. Tearing a small hole in the pillow he drew out stuffing. Around him his three chairs stood in attitudes of reproof.

He was awakened by the sound of the radio turning on in the bedroom. He arose from the living room floor feeling stiff and miserable. He cut himself twice shaving, had no time for a shower. On his way out he felt a new kind of repentance, vague and half-formed. He turned and addressed all his furniture: —You'll see.

He was half an hour late to work. As he entered, a colleague smiled at Blumfeld's bedraggled appearance and said, —Hard night? as if making a joke at his, Blumfeld's, expense, proper Blumfeld. Blumfeld gave him a grim smile, as if to say, what a thing to ask at your age, are we still boys? His colleague stared at him reproachfully—or was it wistfully?

Blumfeld sailed through the day's work with mere competence, on winds of habit, with none of his usual nicety. Normally he attended his figures with the care of a doctor, as if they were signs of a kind of life more definite than his own. An entry of thus-and-so under Miscellaneous meant something quite real to Blumfeld, and he retained figures easily in his memory. But today he was in the grip of something larger. He entered and calculated mechanically, though correctly, as a celebrity might play a benefit concert without giving his utmost. Blumfeld was marshaling his particular genius for some special transaction that he felt sure awaited him.

He lunched out, on a salad and a glass of white wine. As he waited for the check, he analyzed his lust, his shame and repentance. He was ashamed not of his behavior, but because the furniture was not truly his; he rented it with the apartment. He had always rented furnished apartments, because there was a heaviness and a solitude in ownership. He shared the laundry room with other tenants, his car was parked with other vehicles in the underground garage, sounds from the next apartment sometimes penetrated his own—all this, even if sometimes inconvenient or even painful, was to Blumfeld salutary. It kept him connected to the world. He felt indeed that it was good to own nothing, to use only what you needed, holding it in trust as it were for the next user. So it troubled him that he had violated the trust implicit in his furniture. But he was pleased too, because now he saw another kind of trust. Things honestly used acquired an honest luster. Just as he was unquestioned proprietor of the ledger, so he would win the trust of his furniture, and his honest possession of it would enrich it. He left the restaurant filled with conviction, and when he returned to the office he called in his assistant.

—Marianne, I've meant to talk to you about your ledger entries. It won't do, it really won't. Figures transposed, entries in the wrong columns. Mistakes can be corrected, but there is a larger issue. This ledger is a trust. Others who come after us will use it, and we should surpass ourselves in their behalf. Our excellence will inspire them.

Marianne nodded, her eyes wide. For an uneasy moment Blumfeld thought she was humoring him. Then he saw that she was merely in awe of his new strength. He waved her out of the office, and when she had gone he said under his breath, —Whore. It shocked him to say this. It burst on him like an unpleasant truth. Yet no truth is wholly unpleasant. He had seen Marianne ineffectively resisting the advances of salesmen. Her weakness was regrettable, but it couldn't be denied. He felt humbled, for he had seen that truth was a mighty and ungiving master, and he was its servant. With renewed dedication, he returned to his ledger.

That evening as he unlocked his apartment, Blumfeld was approached by the woman who lived next door. He had nodded to her in passing in the hallway, but they had never before spoken. She always dressed in the same severe dark blazer and skirt. Now she wore a pale green housedress, and she was barefoot. Her hair was tousled, her expression mischievous.

—Say, do you have a vacuum cleaner? My husband was horsing around and broke a pillow. There's feathers everywhere.

—No, sorry, said Blumfeld, smiling. —I use the cleaning service.

—So do we.

—Oh, he added, almost winking. —I may rearrange my furniture later. I'll try not to disturb you.

But when he entered he was in no mood of lust. He found it necessary to address his furniture didactically before taking his pleasure. He arranged the three chairs in a semicircle facing the sofa across the glass-topped coffee table. In stocking feet Blumfeld tested the strength of the glass top with his own weight, then climbed up. His voice rose and fell in uneven harangue. By the time he was done he was stripped to his socks. Occasionally he stopped to swig from a bottle of Scotch he had placed on the table. When he descended from his perch, he tied two of the chairs back to back with a sash cord and directed the third chair: —Watch. He tossed aside the sofa cushions and propped the folding bed half open, then knelt before its yawning mouth.

In the morning, Blumfeld was again penitent. He resolved to abstain, though even then he felt the weight of the world upon the frailty of his resolve. He untied the chairs, and as an afterthought arranged them in novel positions around the room. He propped the sofa cushions against the wall. He turned the coffee table on its side, leaning its glass top against the closed drapes. Then he left without studying the result of his work. Upon his return, he decided, he would be able to read in this arrangement the desires of his furniture.

Again he was late to work. Again his day passed in a fog of anticipation. On the way home he stopped at a gourmet shop. When he entered the apartment, the arrangement of his furniture seemed to rebuff him. From his parcel he withdrew wine, paté, and cold fowl. He sat familiarly, but with fondness and even some reserve, on one of the chairs as he spread his meal on the kitchen table. When he finished eating he cleared the tabletop and buffed it with lemon oil.

Then, good intentions forgotten, he behaved again like a brute. He attacked the chairs with a knife, since that was the only way through the seat covers to their innards. He moved about the room. Even the desk, the reminder of work in his home, the one piece of furniture he owned, did not escape his embrace. Near the peak of his passion he hauled on one of the drapes and it came down, exposing the plump white body of Blumfeld as if on a screen to anyone who cared to look. He snapped off the lights and opened the window. He poured the remaining wine over the chair and dropped the bottle out the window. His breath came rhythmically and he worried the slit fabric with his fingers. His feet were braced against the wall.

Friday morning he was possessed by an extreme, over-mastering disgust. His apartment was a shambles. It stank of sweat and sour wine. This madness had gone far enough. He would buy cigarettes and a new book on his way home, and return to his regular habits. He would dine out. He had no time to clean up the mess, so quickly he swept shreds of stuffing into piles, righted a chair, and replaced the sofa cushions haphazardly.

Hastily he dressed. For a moment he considered his frayed cuff, a reminder of the torn fabric of the chair. Although old, his suit was of good material and could last years more. How, he suddenly wondered, did his company sell so many clothes? He realized with something like vertigo that this industry, all industry, was based not on the individual purchase, but on an ongoing stream of purchases, on things wearing out and being replaced over and over without end. The figures in his ledger, then, had no individual significance; their only meaning was in the sum, in the ongoing traffic month after month and year after year. He picked his way around the ruined furniture to gaze out the window at the traffic. Did they know? Cars crawled toward the city, sped away from it. Did they know that, one by one, they were not real, that they counted only in the mass?

At work he was called to the president's office.

—Blumfeld, said the president, you know I never meddle with the private lives of my employees. But there has been talk. I don't intend to credit it, no, idle gossip is useless and destructive, and in any case what you do is your own business. But I will say this. This is an old firm, a traditional firm. In the quality of our clothing, in our business practices, we stand for something. Nowadays we hear a lot about the breakdown of tradition, and I for one take a lenient view. I credit it to ignorance. A lot of people are ignorant of the value of tradition. But a man of your age, Blumfeld—! If what they say is true, so much the better. I know you value tradition, I know your work is impeccable, no, please, this is only your due, and if the talk is true, I know you will behave honorably. There, I've said it, I will say no more. By the way, have you got a new suit?

Blumfeld had stood silently through this, despite his surging emotions. The president was a doddering old fool who spouted homilies and what he was pleased to think of as philosophy. Blumfeld had even, on occasion, defended the president's oratory. Now, though, he was deeply disturbed. It was impossible that the president knew about his furniture. He must have got it into his head that Blumfeld was seeing some young lady, with an eye to renouncing his, to the president, unseemly bachelorhood.

—No, said Blumfeld with an effort, I find that my old suit serves me quite well.

—Yes, that is creditable. A man who values tradition over fashion. But, Blumfeld, we deal in clothes! What impression does your suit make on an outsider? That is the point.

With this the president fell back in his chair, as if utterly exhausted. He pulled open a desk drawer, withdrew a bottle and a tumbler, and poured himself a drink.

—We are to be audited, he said. —The auditor comes Monday. I would consider it a favor, Blumfeld, a personal favor, if you would avail yourself of the employee discount and buy a new suit for the occasion. That's all.

Blumfeld attempted to comply. But when he walked into the fitting room and saw the mannequins frozen in their postures of arrogance, grief, torpor, avidity, deference, three of them limbless and two with limbs askew, he had to leave at once.

In the hallway Marianne stopped him. Her eyes were cast down and her hands worried the hem of her blouse.

—Mr Blumfeld, I've been thinking about what you said to me . . .

—Yes, yes, another time, said Blumfeld harshly. Even though he should tell Marianne about the audit, he was too agitated now to face her awful shyness and self-abasement.

She looked at him with vulnerable eyes. —Yes, another time. I'd like that. Perhaps you can show me what I'm doing wrong. Perhaps this weekend . . .

Blumfeld's amazement must have shown in his face. Marianne cast her eyes down. He felt a rapid succession of emotions: sympathy, power, contempt. Blood burned in his ears, and he stammered, —Well, I . . .

—I understand, said Marianne softly. —You're busy. It's not fair of me to ask for your personal time. She turned and walked briskly away from him.

He drove home faster than was his habit, crossing lanes whenever an opening appeared before him. He steered deftly and without thinking, his lips moving in a rapid undertone. When he exited his tires squealed. At the garage he turned his key in the post and the gate squeaked open.

The elevator was broken. He climbed the seven flights to his apartment, and arrived at his door panting and sweating. He leaned against it for a minute. When he entered, he saw the chaos of cushions, stuffing, draperies and pillows. The smell pushed itself down his throat. He shut his eyes. When he opened them he saw. The colors were rich and warm with meaning. The disarray was articulate and complete. His furniture had at last accepted him. With a muted cry he ran to the window and flung it wide. On the highway, across the broad bowl of the valley where night gathered, cars streamed past, specks of pale color. The lights of airplanes moved on the evening sky. Perched on the sill, he could see that the house on the hill was dark. He sprang from the sill, and he flew. Blumfeld flew. He rose straight up, accelerating, going higher and higher until the world became a blur and his consciousness ceased.

THE MENAGERIE OF BABEL

I was living then in a rundown cottage behind a ramshackle house in Berkeley. It was a single room without electricity or plumbing. My landlord owned and lived in the main house with several other tenants. His name was Peter Fraser. He was a law school dropout with an overbearing manner that collapsed the moment I resisted it. Then he was almost unctuous. In a week, the competition for housing among returning students would be desperate, but he chose to take my cash. I guessed that because of his manner he had trouble keeping tenants. We smoked a joint on the deal, and between lies I told him some harmless truths about myself.

Berkeley was neutral ground for me. When asked, I would say that I had come to finish my master's degree. But once on the road I took every chance to prolong my trip. On my last ride south from Eugene I woke from the shallow dreams peculiar to travel to see with what woe the mud flats of the bay and, across it, San Francisco vague in smog. I knew then that all my intentions had been stories. I had come because there were choices I didn't want to make.

So I have no right to judge Murphy. He too was avoiding life. At every crux of choice stands an angel, and only after you have chosen your path do you see his other face, that of a demon, taunting, vilifying, forbidding return. Glimpse this face, and you live on a rack of doubt. My choice was to live out the folly I had started or run the gauntlet of retreat.

Murphy had no such crises. He was an idiot; I mean, his mind was his own, unique almost to the point of insanity. Unlike me, he had found something to sustain him.

The morning after I moved in I met him in the back yard. He was drawing. His pad was on an easel, and he studied it obsessively as he worked. He was shirtless and pale. His shoulders and arms were freckled. I had never seen anyone so thin. In his left hand was a drafting pen which rattled as he shook it. I had already stepped out of the cottage when I saw him and I almost stepped back in, to preserve my solitude. Perhaps it was the sun burning on the white page and black ink that arrested me. I took the drawing for a sea urchin until I saw his subject there in the yard, a withered sunflower.

He turned then. Where his drawing was severe and remorseless, his features were soft. It was a face almost without character, except for the eyes. In them was a look I had sometimes surprised in myself: a yearning, a need for the touch of another soul so strong that, when repulsed, it quickened to reproach and hurt. His eyes like mine were too ready to offer loyalty and to bruise when brushed aside. We said hello. With the politeness I used to combat my diffidence, I told some small lies, and one truth: I liked his drawing. Sometime I must see more of it. He immediately agreed and invited me to his room. I disliked him for it.

He lived in the cupola of the house. It was filled with potted plants, and with his drawings. A horseshoe crab, a deer skull, cacti, seed pods. They all had the same stark, disconcerting quality. I glanced at them, away from them, as if expecting some transformation, some other world to emerge. Murphy watered his plants. He lifted the lid of a terrarium, and behind a cactus a dun lizard's tail lashed.

—I love these, he said, reaching in to touch a cactus spine.
—Do you know why? They know the secret. Life is a drug.
We'll turn ourselves into anything to have it.

I looked again at the drawings, and all at once they were
morbid. Around the edge of each object was an intense, oblit-
erating space. Every line battled this void. The overdrawn precision was claustrophobic.

He lifted his finger from the spine and regarded the red bead
forming on its pad. Briefly he pressed it to his mouth.

—Why so many? So many types? Who can explain it?

I began to answer by Darwinian rote. But his faint smile
silenced me and forced me to my more authentic belief: the
world was a plenum. His innocent question, if it was that, was
the one thing he could have said to draw me from my politic
silence into a study of him.

The main house was a holdover, or recapitulation, of the com-
munes of the sixties. Dinners were shared, so I gained a quick
if empty introduction to the seven tenants. A nearly pathological
avoidance of questions kept me from learning much beyond
their public stories. One man played bass for a band always about
to get work. One woman studied midwifery. Another was a
proofreader for a Buddhist press. One couple, specialists in "no-
etic research," seemed to do nothing but drift in and out at any
time of the day or night. One day I came back from a walk to
find them peering into my cottage through its one window;
they did not return my greeting. Their eyes were like cold oil.

My landlord liked to complain to me, as if thereby forming
an alliance. I suspect he tried it on all his new tenants. He
confided that he was owed hundreds of dollars in back rent. Yet
as far as I could see he had no other source of income. He went
out in his battered Karmann Ghia only for tennis, movies, and

political meetings. His way of life at least had an easy explanation: he had a trust fund, and sold drugs.

On occasion Murphy took his drawings to Telegraph Avenue
for sale. One afternoon I went with him, because the route
crossed campus and I wanted a look. If the place became real
to me, I might be moved to act. And I needed to buy an oil
lamp. Peter had offered to run an extension cord from the house
to the cottage, but I knew I would be obligated to him for it.
I also wondered how real Murphy's business connection was.
Parts of his life seemed an elaborate fantasy. I had nothing against
this—certainly my own life was largely fantastic and seemed at
times a slow but definite form of ritual suicide—but if I were
to know him I would feel more secure knowing the boundaries
of his delusion.

Murphy and I crossed campus. The buildings had Mediterranean roofs grafted to Beaux Arts facades. They asserted that
culture could be possessed, moved, recombined. But the sunlight disagreed and glared off them like a halo, like the defensive
edges of Murphy's drawings. Girls passed, slit skirts from another
era swinging, on the plaza that a decade earlier had been flooded
with riot police and tear gas. Two streetcorner prophets, not yet
extinguished by the natural selection of social history, hung on
the edge of campus, one reading scripture from file cards, the
other preaching a philosophy of hate. I was not after all badly
matched, in my motives of refusal and escape, to this place of
denied history. I was not without the grace needed to believe
one could start anew.

Murphy's connection was real enough. From a folding table
in front of a record store he sold drawings and photos of local
scenes. He accepted Murphy's rolled sheaf and shook his head.

—My man, why don't you get yourself a matte knife? Now
I have to take these to the frame place and it comes out of your
money.

Murphy shrugged. The vendor counted off several twenties and pushed them across the table. He left his hand on them.

—Listen, you want some coke?

Murphy said no.

The hand came off the bills. The vendor smiled. —Don't tell me you do this stuff straight. Take it in trade sometime, okay?

From here Murphy crossed to a bookstore with an Indian name. He circled the shelves deliberately, pulled down some books, and laid them on the counter. The first title was by Henri Bergson. I started to say something, but as the cashier picked up the rest I was silenced. Flying saucers. Gods. Magic.

—It's bullshit, said Murphy pleasantly as we left the store. —But it's true bullshit. I know you won't agree, you're a biologist.

—What? How did you know? I felt violated. The secret had been easy enough to keep at the dinner table.

—By the way your eye traveled over my drawings.

Not possible. Yet somehow he had known.

—You see, when you look at things . . . He looked around him, as if suddenly discovering he was in the middle of a crowded street. Dancing toward us was a band of Krishnas in saffron robes, banging hand drums and singing. He seemed panic-stricken. —Let's, let's go. Can we take the long way home?

We crossed campus and walked uphill past a stadium and into the hills. We were entering a botanical garden when I heard an insistent shrieking.

—What's that?

—Dogs. The university has labs up here.

We passed succulents, camellias, rhododendrons, eucalypti, sage, manzanita. Murphy stopped by a cactus and broke off a lobe. Gingerly he slid it into his shirt pocket. We entered a stand of sequoia, the ground thick with ferns. Murphy picked a cone from the ground and looked at it curiously.

—They won't grow unless there's been a fire. He said this with wonder, as if he had just discerned it. My sense of time suffered a shift. In the plants, in the shape of these hills, was the sense of a young Earth. Everything looked prehistoric. Murphy turned to me. —You see, if you look at things, after a while something emerges. You find that, that things want to change into other things. And you can draw that. What they were. What they want to become. And in, in people too.

—In people?

He looked at me. —For example, you want to be dead.

I stood appalled. Then I laughed. —Murphy, you're an idiot.

He continued to look at me, appraising me, with no control over his eyes' need. —Yes, they're the ones who, who can't speak.

—What?

—They're at the level of three year olds.

He had read some book on eugenics. —No, it's just, in Greek, *idios*, it means the self, that's all. It means private. Idio-syncratic. That's all I mean.

—Yes. Because an idiot can't be understood. You give up something of your self to be understood. Do you know much about genetics?

I was still not used to his abrupt shifts. —Genetics? No one does, really. They all pretend.

—I read a story once. It was about a library, made of all the possible combinations of letters . . .

—Permutations, yes. The library of Babel.

—You know it! It exists?

—Murphy, it's a story. An intellectual fantasy.

—Yes, but, but DNA is like the letters of the alphabet, its molecules A C T G and, and if you rearrange them . . .

—You could have a menagerie of Babel.

—Yes. Yes, that's right.

—No, it's not right. There are laws. . . . And I stopped.

Whatever the defects of Murphy's popular understanding, this was indeed Darwinism, the possibility that, as Julian Huxley put it, "given sufficient time anything at all will turn up." In its implications it was finally as fantastic as any theory of Murphy's. What laws could give this opening of all possibility any human meaning? No one knew. Not knowing turned the plenum into a chaos.

The function of DNA is to copy itself. Yet it does not, not exactly. When it fails, it creates sports and mutants. By this failure life diversifies, and not, we hope, aimlessly. But we are unable or unwilling to know the laws. If we knew them they would change us.

—This was my work, I confessed. —I majored in genetics.

—You quit?

—I was . . . eased out. Just as well for me.

—But it's important! This is my work too.

—Your work? What do you mean?

—If, if you draw things, if you always use the same kind of line . . . It helps me learn, about growth, about form. That's the only reason I do it.

—That's all? No pride in your art?

He looked stunned. —Pride? In, in copies of copies?

I thought I understood. As if the grandest Chartres could rival the balance of a bumblebee, or the finest pigment ever more than mock the glint of snakeskin.

—But you say that life is monstrous, I said.

—It is.

—Then why draw it? Don't you have to look at things with love in order to see their pasts and futures?

—Yes. That's the worst. I do, I do love all this.

Overhead a firespotting plane droned, crossing and recrossing the dry grassgrown hills. Below us the Bay spread out its bounty under a primal sun. I could see the beasts of Murphy's fancy taking color in this light, living their unthinkable lives, but not on the canvas of his innocence. No, I saw them body forth from genetic laboratories, the same burgeoning industry that my classmates had been so eager to join. Was the world indeed a nightmare of congenital competition, or was there yet some place for cooperation at the center of being? For my own reasons I needed to believe the latter; I needed also, unlike Murphy, to know that I was not deluded in my belief.

—Have you read Rilke? he asked.

—No.

—He says that beauty is the beginning of terror. That every angel is terrible.

—Then why is it beauty?

—Because it suffers us to live.

Now he had touched the core of his obsession, and his lean nervous body shook with zeal. His thin stuttering voice was driven by its force. He spoke of the forces which could thrust up from the same proteins a whale, a hummingbird, or any of a thousand different cacti. He spoke of resemblances among the enzymes of sharks and those of grasses. But if this was a source of wonder to me, to him it was a horror. His world was the fever dream of a mad, insomniac intelligence. But its means were those of Darwinism, which also limited the instruments of creation to permutation and competition.

—All the plants, the animals, all this superabundance, and no reason for it except nature's in, insatiable h, hunger for new forms. This ap, ap, appalling diversity! Life is, is nothing but a freak show! Look at it, just look!

His attempts to find an order were like mine in everything but method. My work too was a heresy against the dogmas of science, though constituted by them. So I did not tell him how constantly the idea of an ordered world had been asserted and assailed, from Plato through Spinoza, Leibnitz, Schelling, Darwin. Its history was a history of failure, though of a kind I aspired to.

—And you, he said, you can help me. You've studied this. I
go to the university library, there are so many books I don't
know where to begin . . .

So. If Murphy would use me to work out his obsession, then
I might use him as proof against delusion. With his idiocy before
me I might be less likely to fall into solipsism. This quid pro
quo, perhaps the nearest thing to friendship I could offer, was
at least a form of cooperation.

One of my friends from Cambridge now lived in Berkeley.
Homi had put me up my first week in California. He was from
New Delhi originally. When I told him about Murphy he
smiled and asked if Murphy was a Krishna.

—I can't think of anything less likely.

—Oh, this horror of life can become quite ecstatic.

And he told me a Hindu legend about Shiva and his consort
Parvati. One day a powerful demon came to Shiva and demanded Parvati. Angry Shiva opened his third eye, and at once
another demon sprang from the ground, a lionheaded beast
whose nature was pure hunger. Thinking quickly, the first demon threw himself on Shiva's mercy, for it is well known that
when you appeal to a god's mercy he is obliged to protect you.
So the anguished lionhead asked, "Now what? What am I supposed to eat?" And Shiva said, "Why not eat yourself?" And so
the lion did, starting with his tail, eating through his groin, belly,
and neck, until only his face was left. And to this sunlike mask,
which was all that remained of the leonine hunger, exultant
Shiva gave the name Kirttimukha, or Face of Glory. He decreed
that it should stand over the doors to all his temples, and none
who refused to honor it would ever come to any knowledge of
him. Those who think the universe could be made another way,
without pain, without sorrow, without time or death, are unfit
for illumination. None is illumined who has not learned to live

in the joyful sorrow and sorrowful joy of this knowledge of life, in the radiance of the monstrous face of glory which is its emblem. This is the meaning of the faces over the entrances to the sanctuaries of the god of yoga, which word is cognate with yoke.

Homi had a hypnotic voice—his accent falling on American idioms was beguiling—and as he spoke I thought of my demonic angels of choice, their twin faces merging into Kirttimukha, sun-faced lion of life, and for the moment I felt at peace.

Before I left, Homi asked: —Have you spoken to . . . anyone back East?

I said no. Seeing me out, he touched my arm.

The next time I saw Murphy he had a fantastic book on human cloning and a practical guide to the grafting of cacti.

More from obligation than desire, I filled out my application to the university, as an earnest that a new life could start for me here. But the first thing the gatekeepers of the future ask is where you come from.

Let me tell you, then, about Paul Kammerer. He was an Austrian biologist who set out to demonstrate the inheritance of acquired traits. This evolutionary doctrine was anathema to Darwinists then and is still. Kammerer forced *Alytes obstetricans*, the midwife toad, to mate in water in order to induce the so-called nuptial pads to form, normally absent in this land-dwelling species. After several generations of mating in water, the darkened pads were present in the offspring. So Kammerer claimed. The only preserved specimen was examined by a hostile critic ten years after its preservation. On examination the darkening proved to be fresh India ink. Kammerer clearly had nothing to do with this botch of a hoax, which proved only that some lab assistant had tried clumsily to help him or maliciously to discredit him. But his critics were to tie the validity

of all his work to the fraud of this one specimen. Disgraced, he
blew his brains out.

No attempt had ever been made to duplicate Kammerer's
experiment. I decided to do it.

My advisor had urged me to work in recombinant DNA. I
demurred, and in one step moved from the cutting edge of my
field to the backwaters of Lamarckism. We will not speak here
of my apparent need to doom myself. I had good reasons as
well. I thought that too many favored Darwin's fiction of life
because it tacitly endorsed every murder as life-furthering. Nor
could I return to Lamarck's earlier myth, that no useful effort
is wasted, that children may inherit the acquired traits of their
parents. It was too wistful and consoling for me to swallow. But
I used it as a name for my ignorance.

For a year I persisted, walking the two miles from our apartment to the labs almost every night, entering between the two
stone rhinoceri, the grates in the quad steaming in all seasons,
the mist forming coronas around the lamps. At last I had my
second generation of *Alytes* and encouraged them to mate in
water, *contra naturam*. I cleaned the fertilized eggs and kept them
alive for two weeks. Then approval for my project was with-
drawn. My incubators were shut off.

Science, like everything else, is a community. The work of
the mind alone with itself is necessary but not sufficient. The
only possible redemption for this solipsism is that the community be able to draw meaning from it. Kammerer failed at the
last step, and I had followed him into the purgatory of the
excluded.

An odd coincidence I discovered later was that Kammerer
shot himself on my birthday. Another was that the son of Kammerer's harshest critic was a regent of the University of California. Kammerer was a collector of coincidences, and I gather
these here only for his sake, and for Murphy, who would doubtless find them meaningful.

———

It is only by a series of accidents that we become what we are. We can look back on the branching paths of cancelled possibility, an angel standing at each branch, that might have led to different selves. What is the number of accidents? What is the shape of necessity? The notion that everything is possible is monstrous, so we restrict, by observing, then defining, then excluding, what does not fit our need. But the excluded remain with us. That which we might have become continues to haunt us.

To me this was the true menagerie, the myriad triumphs and failures of will that make us what we are. Since I hoped that creation was a plenum, I suppose I should have felt the same about choice. But I thought my will imperfect and liable to error. Therefore I admired will-less Murphy. It was the basis of our friendship. Life is the exchange of energies.

In all, I was as much a mother to him as I could be. By degrees he opened up to me about himself. He was born in California. He had never finished high school. He put himself through a trade school by selling commercial illustrations. He worked in numerous small ad agencies, always quitting after a brief time. He had no social life at all, and filled his off-hours by reading von Daniken, Velikovsky, Nietzsche, Bergson, Borges, Frost, Hegel, Heinlein, Ouspensky, Koestler—a chaos of interests. He owned no books on art.

He began a painting, his first. To cadge a glimpse I teased him about not using always the same kinds of lines. He said solemnly, —This is something else. I'll show you when it's done.

He kept the canvas turned to the wall when he wasn't working on it. It left overlapped horizons of colored lines where the wet top edge leaned.

This is the story I do not want to tell: the real reason I came west.

Evolution, competition, cooperation, plenitude: these are stories we tell ourselves to hold back what we dare not embrace. But time and the timebound mind are unforgiving; the excluded are with us always.

I came west because of John Lang. He was a year ahead of me at school. We had the same friends. He introduced me to the other great fiction of the nineteenth century, that of Karl Marx, the grand vision of cooperation as the furthering force of life.

Lysenko had been the Marxist Lamarckian, a great fraud working against all evidence to vindicate the idea that life was not a free-market economy. Even the Soviets at last had to bow to Darwinism, and Lysenko was written out of history. But as a binding fiction of social life—that we can learn, as a species, that our effort is not lost at death, that cooperation strengthens us—it was what I wanted to believe.

When Lang graduated he went straight to work in his father's chemical firm. We made him the butt of our tolerant abuse— poor John, twenty-one and already bourgeois. He was making thirty thousand a year and drove to Cambridge for weekend visits. We would joke with him and nurse him like a sick bird.

I was living then with Joann, a slim dark beauty. For three years we were married in all eyes but the law's. How much I took for granted. She was looking for a future and I wanted nothing but to bury my past. When I returned from my summer job at Woods Hole she was living with Lang. He had quit his job for another in Cambridge. They took me to dinner. As the food arrived I fled, nauseated at the part I had to play, at my ineffectualness, my poverty, my pain.

The next week was comedy, if you like, as I moved from the apartment of one friend to the next, sleeping on living room couches, receiving unsolicited analysis, sympathy, or barely con-cealed scorn.

I resented most that Lang was using her as the flag of his liberation. "Living in sin" was how he put it to everyone but me. I resented and mourned that there was that in Joann to respond to his instrumentalism. I wondered what story I had used to blind myself to the possibility of betrayal. For as Lang reminded me, almost sadly, betrayal is impossible when cooperation is absent.

When I went west, I left behind my books, my plants, the cat I had saved from a neighbor's drowning. I fled lamenting. How could he ever know her as I had?

But if I cannot judge Murphy, how can I judge Lang? He had known what he needed for his life. I had not even known that I was in competition for her.

I bought a radio. Late at night, I listened to static. Sometimes I tuned in talk shows. One night, after a month in Berkeley, I was reading a book on phylogeny, listening in the interstices of my attention to a discussion of UFOs.

—This is true, the voice said. —The Earth was fertilized from space. Aliens came and mixed proteins in the ancient sea, did this for amusement. The history of life on Earth is a catalog of permutations. All fabulous beasts were once real. We can't have imagined them, our imaginations are poor, we can't imagine a number greater than ten. On their world, life is blessed. But here they have made a genetic cesspool. It was a game to them. They are all perfect and identical. They do not die, age, or reproduce. Perhaps they come back to observe us, perhaps not, it doesn't matter. It's a freak show, a menagerie of Babel.

At the word *Babel* I looked up. My eyes rose to the cupola. A light was on there. I saw Murphy pacing back and forth, holding a telephone.

Peter Fraser, our landlord, late of Hastings Law School, conducted a purge of the house on September 23, my uncelebrated birthday. He demanded all back rents by the first of October, or he would start evictions. I drove with him to the Co-op to post For Rent notices, his way of letting the troops know he was serious. Kristin, the student of midwifery, was the only one who took it to heart. I was with Murphy when she came up to ask if he was moving. She had to, she said; she hadn't the cash.

I liked Kristin. She was as flighty as the rest of the household, but she was not so self-involved. She said she needed two more months to finish her training, and if she had the added expense of moving it would mean another year of typing at Cal. Murphy listened to this, then took from his desk a roll of twenties.

—Use this, he said. —I don't need it.

After a speechless second she counted the money, wrote him a note, and promised to repay him by the new year. She did not thank him; her manner implied that thanks would debase his act.

Rents paid, we three were invited by Peter to go hiking with him in the Sierra Nevada. I think he wanted to escape the more immediate repercussions of his decree. Murphy and I agreed to go. Kristin declined. Peter was in a bad mood about that and insisted that we leave that night.

We left just after midnight. Peter kept three backpacks ready to go at all times, each equipped for a week's outing. —This is earthquake country, he explained. —When the Big One hits, I'm hiking into the hills for a week until the madness is over.

We drove in Peter's Karmann Ghia, Murphy in the front passenger seat, me wedged into the back with two of the packs. I was still unused to distances in the West. Hours passed and I slept.

Peter stopped at the crest of the Tioga Road. We stumbled out to relieve ourselves under a half moon high in a sky pale with false dawn. We were alone at a still lake under pines and huge granite domes. My heart raced, my breath was a moon-borne wraith on the thin air.

Day broke as we turned south on route 395. A few miles west of us rose the sheer scarp of the eastern Sierra. As we turned off the highway onto Pine Creek Road, the face of the mountains appeared flat, without perspective. Then the road veered. Peter downshifted. In a few moments the mountains opened and we were among them. Gray shoulders of the range thrust up so steeply that much of them had been shed on talus slopes. One rugged black giant was striated with branching veins of lighter rock.

The road ended at a deserted pack station. A few horses stood unmoving in the morning air. We unpacked the car. The air was sweet, the chill just leaving it. Peter put the car key into a small magnetic case and conspicuously held it aloft before slapping it inside a wheel well. —There's the key. In an emergency any one of us can go for help. Straight down 395 to the ranger station in Bishop.

I had hiked in the east, but it was nothing like this. The trail from the pack station wandered out through sparse pines and over a creek that might have been in Vermont, but to raise your head was to see more mountainside than sky. Soon we reached a cleared grade, up which a dusty road cut endless switchbacks. Across the creek to the south was a mine, its buildings and slurry line silent, ugly, and eerie. We climbed, panting. As the sun reached us, I took off my outer shirt. The road gave out and we went in among pines, and past a sparkling indigo lake.

At the next lake we forded a stream and stopped below falls for a lunch of crackers, sausage, and hard cheese, gazing out over the lake, the peaks beyond it, the sky. We went on, and beyond the lake the trail climbed sharply, and the timber gave out, and we were in a vast rock basin. As well call the moon beautiful.

Survival in this zone was hard. Water-hoarding succulents put forth greens and reds delicate as a baby's fingertips in the sandy lee of rocks. The slender reddish grasses, the black lichens, all these attenuated forms grasped for rootholds against constant wind and winter snow. They seemed made for Murphy and his obsession, but he was impassive. He had not even brought a sketchbook.

We followed a stream uphill that ducked under and over jumbled rocks. The only vegetation was scrub. Finally a long series of switchbacks brought us to a pass. We paused here for the view, and to get our wind. Peter passed around a baggie of nuts, raisins, seeds.

The far side of the pass was a jumble of boulders, dotted by remnants of last winter's snow. It fell away and a thousand feet below us was a lake, its shore broken gray rock, its water almost black. Peter led us across the boulders, traversing them at a level some few hundred feet below the pass. Footing was uneven and uncertain.

—I'm making for that notch, said Peter during a pause, pointing to a break in the ridgeline. —There's a gem of a lake just beyond.

Late that afternoon we made camp at a rockbound pond in a glacial cirque. Peaks ringed us round. For perhaps thirty minues I sat spent and dumb, my limbs leaden. Then miraculously my fatigue vanished. I helped Peter pitch the tent, and fetched water. When the water boiled he tore open three foil packs and stirred their contents into the pot. We ate from plastic bowls. Light drained swiftly from the sky. With night there came a windless silence. I heard my heartbeat, Murphy's breathing, the rustle of Peter's jacket, the crack of a rock slipping down a faraway slope.

We stayed up till stars appeared above the rough silhouette of mountains. The ground still held the sun's warmth but the air was cold. The stars were brilliant. Each moment seemed to bring out more. I spotted the Dippers and Cassiopeia's W, but it took Murphy to identify most of the others. I laughed when he pointed out Camelopardelus, the giraffe. Peter rolled a joint, and he and I smoked and he talked while Murphy lay on his back, watching for meteors.

Peter repined over his evictions. He had been more than fair. But these people had acted in bad faith. It was no favor to anyone to support the irresponsible. How the responsible differed from those who paid their bills I did not ask. He sketched the consequences of his Marxist heresy in a capitalist, normative society: his parents gave him grief for dropping out, his job prospects were nil, he suffered angst. Only in the mountains did he feel free.

I found it hard to like Peter. Like Lang, Peter called himself a Marxist. That seemed to mean that he never made too much profit on rent or dope deals. Still, I shared with him some of my own heresies and failures, insofar as they reflected his, and he was a good listener. I was smoking his dope. We all felt fine.

Peter stood. —Gonna take a dump. Anyone else? I almost laughed. Why, I wondered, are Marxists such scoutmasters?

After Peter left, Murphy spoke softly. He didn't seem to care if I listened.

—I used to think I wasn't human. That I was from a star somewhere. They had left me here, to observe, and they would come to take me back. I liked to study things and this gave me a reason.

I let some time go by before I answered. —Why did you need a reason?

—Because studying would never do me any good. It's okay if you have the money to go to college.

Stung, I said: —I was on financial aid. I didn't have any money.

—But your friends did.

That was true. If I was the token poverty case, the one who

would miss outings and parties because of work-study jobs, still I was in that world, a world that Murphy never had a chance to feel outcast from. And I had willfully turned my back on it.

—Which star? I asked.

—Omega Orionis, he said with no hesitation. —They live in an artificial world orbiting the star. It's a winter star.

—How long did this . . . fantasy last?

—A few years. After a while I just stopped thinking about it.

—When I was a kid, I thought I was some kind of mutant. A genetic sport, you know? We need some story to separate us from our parents.

—I was sent here to study Earth things. I was supposed to be an observer. Not a participant.

Despite myself, I wanted to stretch my arms to him and pull him across the gulf he was creating between himself and humanity. —Murphy. What the hell is your first name?

—Hugh.

—Irish?

—My mother says it's Scottish. She wears orange on St. Patrick's Day.

I laughed. —And what's your father?

—Dead.

—Oh.

—I . . . waited for it. He raped my older sister.

I said nothing.

—Trust isn't like a promise. Nothing was promised. Nothing and everything.

I reached and touched briefly his hand. As if to say, Trust me.

—My first name was his name too.

—Is that why you don't use it?

—I sign the drawings "Murphy". It's kind of a personal secret. You know, as if names gave power? It's silly.

—No. If you know someone's name, in a way you're responsible for them.

—And you, you know the names of so many things, don't you . . .

—Not their true names.

Peter's flashlight beam bobbed closer as he returned.

—Did you see that major meteor?

—No. We were talking about glaciers, I said.

—Well, this is the place for them. You should see Evolution Valley. Mt Huxley, Mt Darwin, Lamarck Col . . . Nature named after natural historians. I'll show you slides sometime. You guys coming to bed? I'm fried.

—Soon, I told him.

—Don't step on me when you come in.

After a minute I said: —Murphy, I heard you on the radio the other night.

He was silent.

—Do you believe all that?

—But you think it's the result of chance, he said.

—Is that so bad? Isn't it a relief that nature is indifferent?

—Do you believe in sin?

I was impressed. He had gone straight to the core of my argument. But I played him out.

—Murphy, I'm an atheist.

—But you do.

—You . . . *saw* that.

—Yes.

I could feel Peter's dope getting its second wind. What place was this? So cold and wild.

—Well, you're right. I do believe in sin. Otherwise evil is simply misunderstanding. I don't believe that.

—Then what is sin? he asked.

—A violation . . .

—Of what?

—Of the natural order. What an effort it was to say those words. To admit my belief in a wholeness.

—So there is an order.

—Maybe. Yes, I think there is one, under all the fictions we impose. So there's sin. You're responsible for your actions. Congratulations, you've discovered God. But let me tell you about Occam's razor.

—Yes, you see, that's where the God argument fails. He wouldn't have made . . . all this.

—But why replace him with a race of aliens?

Oh, I was stoned. I could almost see them.

—God is supposed to be good. But if we're of their making, then we can never transcend ourselves, the defects in our material, but only aspire to, to find the controlling form. To know them. And I, I'm still afraid of what I might learn about them.

—Afraid to learn . . . ? By drawing? Then give it up.

—I have no choice!

I saw one of my angels at a crossroad, but this angel was not fearsome. No, this one had trapped himself, and turned slowly with a stricken lost look, while around him a chaos of beings boiled, warred, loved, died, endured.

—Murphy, listen. This chaos all around us, the stupid and the intelligent accept it as order. But you, you wake up suddenly, you see it as it is. The inherent vice in creation. You can't accept it, you can't avoid it. You're doomed. There's no help for you.

—Of whom are you speaking?

—Of myself. Of whatever it is we share. I woke up too. Perhaps it's best for us to choose it.

—Choose to be doomed?

—To be excluded from the charnelhouse.

Murphy stared at the stars. —I'll stay up awhile. Until Orion rises.

———

In the morning we were up at dawn. I left the tent first and walked to lakeside. A fringe of ice spread an inch or two from rocks into the water. The air was cool and lucid with a slight steady breeze. Pink mare's tails swept overhead. Peter came out and regarded the sky. He poured granola into three bowls and laid out climbing gear. He tried to entice us to tackle a rock face with him, tried against his declared politics to catch us by competition. But Murphy and I cooperatively demurred. Instead we two mapped a hike over the pass to another lake.

—Take a poncho, said Peter. —We may get dumped on.

From the pass we descended and left the trail. Across a bowl ringed by peaks we hiked. Murphy stooped once to examine some lichen, burnt orange and black on the gray rock, that strange collaboration of the simplest animal with the simplest plant.

When we stopped for lunch the sky was overcast. A moist wind came steadily from the west. An hour later the temperature dropped. We were about five miles from camp when it started to flurry. All at once the indifference of nature was no comfort to me.

—Let's go back.

—It may blow over, Murphy said.

—Let's go back while we can.

We almost missed the trail. The surrounding mountains had vanished. A few inches of snow had collected. Wind gusted from the direction of the pass, billowing a thick white curtain all around us.

—Christ.

—It's that way, said Murphy calmly.

—I know. But you can't see fifty yards.

—What should we do?

—I don't know. I think we should go down.

—It's a long way to the road.

—At least it's downhill. Maybe we can get below the snow.

—Do you think so?

—I don't know.

—What about Peter? We should go back to the tent.

—It's miles! We have to climb into the storm, over the pass, and do you remember that boulder field? Could we cross it in this?

—Whatever you want.

We were not dressed for this. The morning had been mild. I wore a shirt, sweater, poncho, and wool cap. Murphy wore a light down parka. Snow, caked around my boots, was melting into my socks. My toes stung. I could feel my sweat chilling as we stood there.

—We can make it to the road by dark, I insisted.

But that was not our luck. Crossing the stream below, Murphy lost his footing and soaked himself to the knees. The snow increased. Wet and heavy, its runoff swelled the stream. When we reached the next ford, Murphy balked. Rocks flumed the water, cast up pearls of foam.

—Maybe we should go back, Murphy said.

—Damn it, we're committed! I could see perhaps twenty yards. Beyond that all vanished. —We can't cross here. Give me the map.

He shrugged out of his day pack, unzipped it, and handed me the folded topo map. Farther on the trail met the stream again. We might traverse the arms of the trail's U and avoid a crossing.

—Look. We can stay this side of the stream most of the way. We cross at Upper Pine Lake, pick up the trail and follow it down.

Shivering, he stared at the rushing stream. —Whatever you want.

We slipped on snow-covered rocks. Occasionally I glanced back at Murphy's lagging figure. Then a panic jolted me. I could no longer hear the stream. I looked at my watch in disbelief.

An hour had passed since we left the trail. At best an hour of light remained. Staring at the map I tried to think.

Murphy, marching numbly on, bumped into me. He went to his knees, and I grabbed him. He swayed while I picked up the sodden map. It came to pieces in my hand. A cold gust took the scraps and blinded me. The snow was now hard and stinging.

—Now? said Murphy.

I chose a direction. After five minutes I felt sure that we were going downhill. We jostled against one another. I heard a growing roar. We had found the stream, or, no, another, surely another, for before us was a moonsharp cliff, impossible to descend, water booming and cascading over the lip. I turned us before Murphy saw. He stumbled against me, his voice a moth in my ear: —Now?

A memory of his voice reached me: *You want to die.* In despair I looked up, as if to summon the sun. Murphy too looked up. Then he raised his arm and shouted: —Look! Look there!

I squinted into the chaos. Light was fleeing into the nothingness.

—They're here!

I was enraged that he should debase our deaths with his hallucinations. I stumbled, then sat in the soft snow, thinking that this, being a voluntary act, might cure him. Dimly it came to me that I need not get up. He was right, I did want it: a clean death. And I had brought him into it.

He began to sing.

From the dusk emerged two figures. They were hikers. It was coincidence they had come, lost as us, just as Murphy's insanity began. I made a murderous effort in every muscle to rise and didn't move at all.

—Help us, I said.

The taller man, rime-bearded, shook his head leisurely. He smiled. They went on into the snow. Murphy gave a cry and ran after them. Another gust blinded me. In my anger I thought, Let him fend for himself.

I began to dream. I dreamed that Murphy and I were seated crosslegged in the snow, reciting the true and secret names of every species of life. Each name brought about the extinction of a species. The world became sparer and more orderly. We chanted outside of time, beyond death and strife and chaos.

When I emerged into a pellucid state of waking, Murphy was beside me. He must have run in a circle. The wind had fallen. I felt warm and relaxed. Sparse large flakes dropped straight down. It was dark, but above us the ghost of a moon raced through clouds.

Then the dark was riven by a roar and a gyre of light. Its bite was as clean as the cold and as real. I felt time snap like a dry twig up its length. My angels, my demons, stood at the fork. Live or die, they cried. Choose, choose. Their grins were great as stars. I turned to hide, but the light went through me. I saw Murphy, the green of his parka beneath drifted snow, the blue of my sleeve flung over him, his face a relief in the fierce light. I turned again into the brilliance and roar. And then I knew. These were not my demons. They were his.

—Spaceship, I whispered. I could deny it only with my voice, not with any force of mind. Then I saw that my word had brought it closer. In a gust the great ship rocked, its engines labored, its light danced, as if biting deeper into reality. I had imagined myself in some grace of the excluded, but now I knew that it had all counted, every word, every evasion. A choice not made was still a choice. Now I was called to account. Some acid of life they would use on me. In the sterile steel cirque of the vessel, they would parse me, reduce the irreducibles of my genes, and make me new. Death was not my fear. The prospect of a changed life was. And the singing in the air was: Choose!

I raised my arm to signal them. I owed him this.

The glow came down. A hatch opened. I saw the suited figures emerge.

I returned to Berkeley two days later. They had taken us to a hospital in Reno. Twenty-four hours later I caught a flight to Oakland. Peter stayed with Murphy, who was still in poor condition.

The house was empty. I sat alone in the living room until Kristin came home from work, and I told her what had happened, from the start of the storm until the Forest Service helicopter picked us up just before dawn.

Toward the end of my story I lost control of my voice and began a compulsive, erratic biography. She listened to everything I had so carefully secreted since arriving in Berkeley, and to things I had not myself remembered in years. I raved for thirty minutes. I ended: —Darwin at the age of sixty received from Marx an inscribed copy of *Das Kapital*. He never read it. He thought the German language was ugly. It's all right now. I'm better. I can stop now. I'm sorry. I can stop now.

But I could not face the cottage. So I slept in her bed that night. She said that I woke once, about three, and shivered for ten minutes. And once in that night lost to my memory she said I mourned: —Joann! Our child. Our lost child.

In the morning, after Kristin left for work, I went to Murphy's room. On the floor below his, a low hum stopped me. The door to the silent couple's room was ajar. I pushed it open. The room had been trashed. Flies made the hum. In the middle of the floor, with a torn strip of sheet round its neck, lay Peter's cat. Its eyes were alive with ants. I lifted the small stiff body and carried it downstairs. I buried it behind the cottage. When I was done I squatted there watching a snail ascend the stalk of a sunflower.

Then I climbed to Murphy's room. In the terrarium a lizard lurked. It darted when I tapped the glass. The dirt in the cactus pots was dry. After a minute I went to the far wall and turned over Murphy's canvas.

It was a Garden, a menagerie. If Rousseau had had the form-haunted medieval mind of Bosch he might have painted it. Disparate limbs conjoined in monsters. Murphy's draftsmanship had made them seamless wholes: haunch joined to fin, mandible to forearm, by the grammar of his line. The flora were likewise impossible. Tree ferns fruited in birds. The flowers of cacti bloomed in strange letters.

It was unfinished. The negative space he marshaled so carefully in his drawings was spread throughout the canvas in patches and voids, as if holding off an unthinkable completion. Near the center stood his aliens: insectile, alike, expressionless, presiding over their creation. Around them were haloes of color, as if he had gone over and over their forms and had not got them right.

A day later he was back. He moved listlessly, like a ghost. There had been tissue damage in his hands. They had nearly amputated. He spent his days reading. We didn't speak.

I tore up my application to the university. The next week I moved out, leaving for him a short farewell verse from Rilke, which I hoped I could myself follow: *There is no place that does not see you; you must change your life.*

But it turned out that I was wrong, that even our selfless acts have secret motives. In my pack, after I left, I discovered on a scrap of paper his reply: *All life is love, and love perishes.* And I knew then that whatever had sustained him was dead.

So I recognized at last the yoke of self, the evolutions of being which bind us and render all our best efforts void and thus free us. Did I think he had used me? No, I had used him, and finally not kept our compact. I had mothered him by cradling my arms to myself and cooing stories for my own benefit, ending by betraying him. By choosing the charnel house for us both. I had taken from him the fiction he needed in order to live. I had sacrificed him to save myself.

And that I could face even this manifestation of Kirttimukha I took for my own strength and purpose. I returned east to fight. Life is the exchange, the unknowable, unnameable exchange of energies.

The two hikers who passed us had been found dead a hundred yards away.

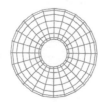

A DRAFT OF CANTO CI

IN HIS LAST MOMENT

SNAPSHOT: THE aesthetic of the accidental.

In a delta Phalos waited for dawn.

In Bangkok Phalos came in the mouth of a Thai whore.

At a service Phalos heard Psalm 106 recited, and at a certain line the chaplain was unable to continue, and had to be led away.

Rotors beat back the grass around him as Phalos crouched beneath a descending copter.

An incoming shell burst a stack of body bags, and the air was filled with a charnel stench.

In the cloudcrested sky the bright dead moon sailed like a sleek craft.

He remembered the swallowtailed wake of the transport, bringing him here, white at dusk.

At the edge of a runway Phalos huddled, shells pounding the strip, his shadow rising behind him.

In a clearing Phalos entered the courtyard of a fallen Annamese wat. From every direction melodies rippled. An array of wind chimes hung round the margin of the court, bronze plates green with corrosion. He tilted his head to the sun and let it blind him, heard the wind speak.

In a canteen Phalos received for cash a packet of heroin.

At leisure Phalos read translations of poetry made by an American fifty years before. In one of these he discovered, by chance, the etymology of his name. It meant not the male organ, but the spike of a helmet, or the first green tip of a sprouting bulb. Accented differently it meant radiant, white.

In the jungle a ball of white phosphorescent gas dogged Phalos's steps.

In his dreams Phalos experienced nothing, nothing at all.

PHALOS HAD A VISION

Everything looks beautiful except there is no star in sight. It is just not visible.

Roger. Is this for star Zero One?

That's correct.

You are not getting any reflections or anything like that that would obscure your vision, are you?

Well, of course, the earth is pretty bright, and the black sky, instead of being black, has a sort of rosy glow to it, and the star, unless it is a very bright one, is probably lost somewhere in that glow, but it is just not visible. I maneuvered the reticule considerably above the horizon to make sure that the star is not lost in the brightness below the horizon. However, even when I get the reticule considerably above the horizon so the star should be seen against the black background, it is still not visible.

Roger, we copy. Stand by a minute, please.

Eleven, this is Houston. Can you read us the shaft and trunnion angle off the counters?

I will be glad to. Shaft 331.2, and trunnion 35.85.

Roger, thank you.

It's really a fantastic sight through that sextant. A minute ago, during that automaneuver, the reticule swept across the Mediterranean. You could see all of North Africa absolutely clear, all of Portugal, Spain, southern France, all of Italy absolutely clear. Just a beautiful sight.

Roger, we all envy you the view up there.

But still no star.

OF A SENTENCE, STRETCHED LIKE A CLOUDCRESTED WAVE OF SKY

Anonymous in guttering torchlight the scribe touched style to papyrus. All these the products of the Earth, himself as well. He drew the ideograms with care: feather, coiled rope, shepherd's staff, loaf, lyre, asp, mouth, owl, twisted rope, loaf, arm, shoulder, seated woman, shepherd's staff, loaf, mouth, bolt, loaf, seated woman, vagina. He paused in the midst of his love poem, a sudden chill of fear piercing him through the summer night. She was no longer here. Yet he pursued his penisolate magics. His fear deepened into dread as he studied what he had written. The signs were not her, yet they were. The same signs differently placed would be something else. In the margin he sketched her features. He was practiced and sure with the ideograms, but he had not the visual syntax to make her likeness in line. Weary, he returned to his poem and finished it, appending his sign: a human figure surmounted by an ibis head. He extinguished the light. For a moment he regarded the moon, then unclasped his skirt and laid on the pallet, praying surcease from thought.

OVER ALL EXISTENCE: EXTENT, DURATION, KAIROS, CHRONOS:

I speak by grace of Mnemosyne. At Hellmouth I paused: within, my love. The wind spoke through my lyre's taut strings, tuned in the Doric mode, the mode of strength and tradition. There the timegod's son spoke out of air, brandished in unseen hand the key to turn me back. There the charnel smell. But I sweetened the air with my tones, with *hypate, paramese, nete, mese, paranete, lixanos, parypate, trite,* and again *hypate,* in nines the counting, the sacred three tripled to suspend time. The god fell back. Then I passed the thin shades, who fell silent at my song. With tones I drew my love from the impure air and led her back to the light. Then foul Aides, detuner, tempered my ninth string with his breath, the earth string, and, facing out Hell-mouth, I paused and struck it. My love dissolved, and I was griefmad, waited seven days at the riverbank for death to take me, and was refused. A second time. A second time I had lost her. So I changed all that I was, broke lyre and sang then in the new modes, unceasingly, a danger to the state as the philosopher rightly said. I took to my bed young boys. I chanted paradise, and was dismembered. But the new modes transcend death, the modes had stopped the maenads' rites, disrupted the ancient cycle, and I did not die. I realized then that they wanted to die. I floated on the sea, my severed head, and learned there songs of tide, *thalassa, thalassa,* came at last to rest with my tongue on foul sand, stopped. A woman came. She tongued sand from my mouth, and empty of music I spoke:—What place?

—Lesbos, she said.

THROUGH WHICH HE SWAM, TO THE EDGE OF THE
MEDIUM, TO THE VOID, OUTSIDE THE FIELD OF
METAPHOR AND FICTION,

Then Father made the cowsuit to satisfy her unnatural lust.

Then made he the labyrinth to contain the offspring.

Then made he the birdwings to free us from the secret that he alone knew.

Did Minos temper the wax sent to the workshop? It is possible. Father showed me his calculations, worked with the Phoenician marks, and the wings were sound. I trusted the figures, and flew no higher than they allowed, assuming of course the wax was good. Minos was deep in debt with his expensive gadgets, and he trusted none, but I did not expect he would temper the wax. Father dwindled from eaglesize to gullsize beneath me. I broke through the cool clouds, like a ghost passing through a pearl, and was staggered: the sun above! Then the wings loosened. A superstitious fear took me, for had I not tried to mount heaven? But my eyes were open even as I fell, and there were no gods. I remember that quite clearly. There were no gods, there in the high places.

AND IN THAT HARD ICARIAN LIGHT WAS BURNED
AND FELL UNNOTICED INTO WAITING SEA,

"There is so much that the United States does not know. This war is proof of such vast incomprehension, such tangled ignorance, so many strains of unknowing, I am held up, enraged by the delay needed to change the typing ribbons, so much is there that ought to be put into young America's head.

"I don't know what to put down, can't write two scripts at once. The necessary facts come in pell mell, I try to get too much into ten minutes. Condensed form is all right in a book; saves eyesight. The reader can turn back and look at a summary.

"Maybe if I had more sense of form, legal training, God knows what, I could get the matter across the Atlantic. . . ."

Words snatched from the air by a shortwave receiver. In a ship offshore three men listened to the speech. One transcribed it in shorthand. One worked the controls of a German-made wire recorder. One smoked. They were preparing evidence for a bill of treason. It was July of 1942.

WHILE THE ENERGY OF THAT SENTENCE

Johann Gutenberg in the city of Mainz in the year 1447 oversaw the hurried printing of an astrological calendar. An assistant stacked the sheets on drying racks. Nearby stood a bored young man, moonfaced and well-dressed, wearing a gold chain clasped with a caduceus at his larynx. He waited to discuss with Gutenberg a debt to his employer, Johannes Fust. He began to speak, then stopped. He touched his lips, then his chain.

It had just occurred to him that these sheets could be sold at market.

LEFT THE WORLD ASHEN

In some other time, these voices called:

I made a list of 20 different products and force-ranked them according to several different criteria. I was looking for something that you could only do online, something that couldn't be replicated in the physical world. I picked books.

Attention itself can now be sold.

When all the world becomes a computer and all the world's cultures are recorded on a single tribal drum, the fixed point of view of print culture becomes irrelevant and impossible, no matter how valuable.

Meant to end with one hundred. The Paradiso. But there is no ending. I cannot make it cohere.

AS THE AFTERMATH OF TORCH TOUCHED TO FOREST,

In the cavity where invention gestates, these voices cried:

Thus they were defiled with their own works, and sent whoring with their own inventions.

And the black sky.

These are the products of the earth: metals, and plants, and those things refined from each, for instance paper and pigment. Food and all the items of commerce are of the earth, and the instruments of war, art and science. And men, too, are of the earth.

Then let us sing in the new modes, and breach technology singing as a son would sing of his father, of the loss of one's flesh.

Then the wings loosened.

For fourteen years confined. The cage.

Remember: the first written signs were those of commerce.

No element is found pure. It is impurity gave birth to solid state electronics. Invention proceeds from impurity. Bring whores for Eleusis. Let *techne* sleep with *praxis*.

Remember that the first tools for graving stone were apt also for murder.

Locked in he wrote with an ink compounded of his own blood and excrement with a sharp tool provided him for his self-destruction on the only foolscap available, namely his own body, those parts of it he could reach.

No picture is made to endure or to live with, but it is made to sell and sell quickly.

The sequence of material is this: fire, air, water, earth. The sequence of life is this: water, air, fire, earth. In spirit the sequence is: earth, water, air, fire, and there is also a fifth element of the spirit: void.

Do not move. Let the wind speak.

SCIENCE TO LOVE,

Claude Garamond observed critically the craftsman's tap of the pyncheon into the type matrix. He pointed out an error in the tail of the upper case Q and the craftsman took down a fresh block of steel and clamped it in his vise. He began again to cut the form with his tools of tempered earth. A printer brought proofs and unfurled them proudly.

—*Maître, les formes sont bien faites. Que pensez-vous d'elles?*

—*Bien,* said Garamond, flicking his gaze over the sheets. —*Celles-ci iront bien.*

—*Et le texte? Que pensez-vous de cela?*

—*Le texte? Je ne le lis pas.*

WORD TO WORLD,

In the asylum sat the poet surrounded by squirrels. The morning sun fell through trees across his shawled legs.

He peered in the direction of the Potomac. He whispered:

—Finding scarcely anyone save Monsieur de Rémusat who could understand him. . . .

The visitor, a young man with an earnest, fanatic's eye, came quietly across the tended lawn.

—Mr Pound?

The poet jerked his head around. The squirrels fled.

A VISION CONVEYED FROM LABORATORY TO JUNGLE,

Monsoon from the south had stopped the filming. The crew was dysenteric, and a month out of pocket in their salaries. The rented army equipment had returned to the capital for a revolution. The director watched the thickening rain, and thought: The accidental is the aesthetic of photography.

He arranged his actors on the steps of the wat. He summoned the lights, the cables, the cameras on their cranes hooded with clear vinyl. Rain glanced on wind chimes in the vast court. American weapons, unloaded, were shouldered by extras. He raised his arm.

One hundred blankfaced Thais waited for his arm to fall.

ITS OBSCURE CHEMISTRY ELUCIDATED IN THE WHITE
GLARE OF JELLIED FIRE.

("A second time? Why? man of ill star.")

On the first day of his reenlistment Phalos led a patrol into
a sector many times captured and lost. His thoughts were obscure. He walked with the dead. But it was his fear that upon
returning to his country he would find it dead that had kept
him here. He would bring out of this place that which he loved.
So the place was the same, and yet not the same. It had been
sprayed with defoliant, and the vines had rotted, the trees shed
strips of their flesh, and leaves exploded underfoot. All gave off
laboratory hues and odors. At night a cool blue fire was seen
here, in globes and streaks, as if souls fled a stinking swamp.
Chatter of automatic weapons forewarned ahead. Behind him a
drone typed for Phalos the aircraft approaching. He turned to
see. Making a run. Payload. The nomenclature of war was vivid
and precise. As the craft closed he saw the markings of his country. Around him the entire squad turned, and yelled.

Fire fell from the sky. Phalos was a pyre. In his last moment
Phalos had a vision of a sentence, stretched like a cloudcrested
wave of sky over all existence: extent, duration, *kairos, chronos*:
through which he swam, to the edge of the medium, to the
void, outside the field of metaphor and fiction, and in that hard
Icarian light was burned and fell unnoticed into waiting sea,
while the energy of that sentence left the world ashen as the
aftermath of torch touched to forest, science to love, word to
world, its obscure chemistry elucidated in the white glare of
jellied fire.

> *"His horse's mane flowing*
> *His body and soul are at peace."*

ALTAMIRA

A FAINT drumming of rain was it? drew Bernard Vogel's attention upward, to a frosted skylight, until he placed the sound as some power tool, deep in the bowels of the Louvre, driving forward the endless renovation. He sighed and looked again at the Madonna of Chancellor Rolin by Jan van Eyck. In the center of the canvas, between the upraised arms of the Chancellor and the Christ child, were two small figures leaning over a parapet. They faced away and watched a river flow past, oblivious to the Virgin within and her veneration by Nicholas Rolin of the fifteenth century.

The two small figures, nearly lost against a vista of houses, steeples, fields, hills, forest, and the opaque light of the sky, troubled Vogel. He could not make them fit. Peacocks walked the parapet. The Child had an aged face, and wore a jeweled cross on his breast. His genitalia were in shadow. Rolin, tonsured and pious, supplicated.

It was conventional for the donor to appear as priest or supplicant. The anachronism was permitted because such scenes were said to be superterrestrial. But van Eyck's art defied the convention. The rendering of Romanesque arches, a walled garden, and the river—certainly of Liege and not of the New Jerusalem—was meticulous. The unity of space and time, coalesced in perspective and light, placed the scene firmly in the real world of bodies, weight, age, and enigmas resolved not by divine grace, but by human craft. *Als ich chan*—as best I can—was Jan van Eyck's motto and signature.

Outside the privileged time of the painting, the principals would rise and leave the studio, van Eyck would touch up, clean his brushes, varnish the panel. This was all the manipulation of materials. No hint of the elusive *Zeitgeist*.

Vogel was weary. For seven years he had taught art history, and would continue to do so, said the board of governors of his college, only if a book was forthcoming. His fellowship and sabbatical were almost over, and he was no closer to a book than when he had flown out.

He was a fair scholar, but he had grown a little dull. Like his friend Cole, he had started with the modern. Like Cole, his scholarship had drawn him back in time. Now his subject was the iconography of the Northern Renaissance; Cole specialized in the Venetian republic. But Cole at least had maintained some sense of living art, distinct from cultural history. Cole would have had at least an inspired guess about the two small figures.

Vogel's feet ached. He sat. He shut his eyes so as to put his mind to rest, but instead it veered to the caves of Altamira. The line drawing of the bison. The anthropologists had not known. For years they argued whether it was fake. But the young Picasso had known at a glance. They were his precursors. In *Guernica* he had placed a Magdalenian bull. Cole had written on it.

If the continuity of art could stretch twenty thousand years, what could Vogel hope to learn from his narrow scholarship? He longed for one glimpse at the heart of his subject. He lived a weak romance, the romance of temporal distance, the fiction that because we have memory the past is accessible. Van Eyck's mind, the motive force, was closed to him.

Yet there must be a memory past memory. Picasso had had it, to see the life in the cave paintings.

Vogel suddenly had a notion about the two figures and opened his eyes. The museum was gone. In its place was a dusty yellow light, spilling into a dim enclosure. He heard the rainy clucking of hens, and the deep moist snort of a horse. It was hot. He sat on a scratchy hay bale. From the gloom his eyes picked out the details of a barn. The dung scent rose up around him.

He had a sensation of entrapment, as if he were dreaming through a false awakening. He rose and walked outside, expecting Paris to crash back upon him in a moment. But outside was a deep still noon, drowsing under a scathing light. Fields stretched to the horizon. He walked until he reached a dirt road deeply marred by hoofprints. Haystacks bordered its flat length, spaced by a hundred meters or so. Far off, a single figure walked the road. Vogel hid behind a haystack. He searched his pockets. He had four marks left over from Munich, seven guilder from Brussels, twenty-some francs in change, more in paper, and two hundred dollars in traveler's checks.

The man walking was a monk, Dominican by his habit. As he passed, Vogel stepped out. The monk raised his arms with a sigh. —Nothing . . . twenty miles back . . . That was all Vogel understood.

—Never mind, Father, said Vogel in halting Dutch. —Can you tell me where I am?

—This is the Bruges Road, said the monk, lowering his hands.

—Bruges?

—Madman, thief, it's all one, the monk muttered in Latin.

Vogel knew Latin a little better than Dutch. He tried it. —What land is this?

The monk regarded this new madness warily. —Flanders.

—And the year?

The monk stepped back a pace and crossed himself. —Anno Domini 1430.

It seemed to Vogel his heart shed a shell. He did not dare think how impossible it was. He was a few miles from the living van Eyck. The light, of course, should have told him. He breathed as he hadn't in seven years.

—Thank you. Thank you. Here, if you've been robbed, perhaps, here, take this . . .

The monk touched the aluminum francs in Vogel's palm, then pulled back as if burned. He went off down the road at a trot.

Vogel stood a moment, then shouted, laughed, and flung the handful of worthless coins into the air.

By the time he reached Bruges his ebullience was gone. He was broke, dirty, and very oddly dressed. After a few tries he found someone who listened to his modern Dutch and gave him directions to the ghetto. The pawnbroker eyed him suspiciously. Vogel explained he was a Spaniard, recently arrived in Bruges, just held up, and that his gold pocket watch, engraved New Haven Conn, was a recent Italian invention. The broker stared at him levelly and said a word in Hebrew. Vogel pretended not to understand. He got ten florins on the gold. The broker wrote on the ticket: *Bernard de jood.*

Vogel spent two days in the market, listening to conversations, observing manners and styles of dress, getting a feel for the actuality of a world that he might never have studied, for all the use that study was to him now. In his hostel at night he practiced the idiom and refined the story he meant to tell. He bought a cheap suit of workman's clothes. He felt unprepared, but he had no more time. His ten florins were almost gone.

Van Eyck's shop was well known. The artist was not in when Vogel arrived. He told a companion that he was Bernardus of Spain, a journeyman applying for work. His features could pass him for a Spaniard, but beyond that his story was ridiculous. He was too old, his haircut was absurd, his accent was puzzling, and his comportment was from nowhere. The companion said Vogel seemed to be a fool and a liar, but they were shorthanded since the shop's move from Lille, and if Vogel didn't do any damage, they would take him on for a pittance.

He was put to work mixing lacquer for van Eyck's temperas.

Nothing could have been more dull. Here, if you could see it from that other world, was Vogel's book: the moment in European art when tempera gave way to oil as a medium. He was in the very workshop where it took place, and he might as well have been sweeping floors in a Cistercian monastery. Jan would not permit apprentices in the shop when he worked, and the brief glimpses Vogel stole at panels were quickly broken:

—Get to work, you!

So he did. After a month his Dutch was fluent, he was expert in purifying linseed and nut oils, and he had lost ten pounds. But the hundred questions he had for van Eyck died on his tongue. Even the companions kept silence around the master. It occurred to Vogel that he might be here for a long time.

Eyck wanted a lacquer that did not need to be set in the sun to dry. His last panel had cracked from the heat. Vogel was the only one in the shop who really took up the task. Within a month he had made a good oil lacquer. But still Eyck showed no interest in trying out oil as a medium for paint. Vogel was beside himself with frustration. One night he entered the shop after the rest had left. He meant to experiment, not so much with the medium, as with his role in this time. Perhaps he was a catalyst. He would dabble with some oil-based paints, then spring the technique on van Eyck.

He sat before a primed wood panel and mixed the ground pigments with linseed oil until he had a workable medium. Vogel had been a respectable draftsman in college, but he had not drawn or painted for ten years. He was interested now in the science of oils, not the art of painting. But he became engrossed.

The feel of the colors under the brush, the presence of sleeping Bruges outside, an almost tangible sense of time in the night air, moved him on. He painted.

Hours passed. In the street the watch cried two. His right thigh was asleep. The painting he had made was not good, but he felt purged. A Madonna, quite rough, but the colors active and fine, the forms showing hints of Matisse over the medieval subject, some muddiness in the folds of the robe . . . he stepped back for a better look, and stumbled into van Eyck standing behind him.

—You are like a demon, Bernard. It is the middle of the night, I see the lamp, I come in, and here is this fiend, arms flailing, painting a hellish picture. I stood for a good ten minutes watching you.

—I'm sorry.

—The student is impatient.

Vogel felt shamed and said nothing.

Van Eyck touched the wet picture and rubbed the color between two fingers while his eyes traversed the panel.

—If you like this sticky stuff you're using, there are better ways to mix it.

—It's, it's a new medium.

—Did you think so? There may be hope for you. Tomorrow I'll put Ruggieri mixing the lacquers, and we'll teach you how to draw. This we burn.

He picked up the panel with his dirtied hand and scaled it into a corner of the room.

First the *paideuma* of materials. Van Eyck did not let him lift a pencil for a month. Instead he read. *Accipe semen lini et exsicca illud in sartaigne super ignum sine aqua. . . . Omnia colores sive oleo sive gummi tritos in ligno ter debes ponere. . . . De oleo quomodo apatur ad distemperandum colores* . . . At times he was moved to protest. —But I know this already.

—It won't hurt you to go over it.

Learning to draw did hurt. Habits of the hand, acquired in another world, had to be unlearned. Usually Eyck would burn Vogel's work without comment, but once in a while he would regard it for a time and say something almost personal.

—When you come home from travel, everything looks strange, yes? Each object in its mire of time. Separate, needing to be brought together again, into this light of the moment of making, yes? Time is a lie. I think you have traveled far, Bernard. In that, you remind me of Hubert.

—Hubert? Vogel the historian was excited. Hubert van Eyck! What a book that would be. —Your brother Hubert? What can you tell me about him?

—Hubert? Hubert is dead, Eyck said dismissively. He came to where Vogel worked and straddled a bench.—Here is what I have to say about Hubert. He was a craftsman. When you are a craftsman they treat you like a shoemaker.

—But the altarpiece at Ghent . . .

Jan looked at him sharply. —What do you know of that? That is work I must finish. But I will do so as an artist. And I will sign my name to it, yes, and Hubert's as well. Bernard, sign your work. Let them know who you are. We are the true aristocrats of the age, you know. That's why I have my own ducal motto: *als ich chan*. Meaning, to my patrons, I can and you can't.

Vogel lowered his eyes. His admirable Johannes, the modest craftsman, had vanished. This man had an ego.

—We are the makers, said van Eyck sadly. —We see for them. And still they will not know me for a hundred years. But for now at least, I am done traveling. I want a good house here, with a stone front. Perhaps you too, Bernard, are done traveling? Is it time to draw these fragments together?

Vogel advanced to drawing in silverpoint, and to backgrounds in tempera. In Eyck's curriculum was no ego. A painter made pictures from the products of earth, just as God had made man from clay. But pictures were base, without permanence. The media had inherent vice; colors faded, lacquers flaked. That was the battle. The painter simply did his best, struggling as in life he struggled against the taint of original sin, without conceited hope of heaven. Real gold in the gold leaf, not because the guild might check, but because purity of technique was a holy office.

—You know, said Vogel one day, —I think these oil colors will last longer than tempera.

Van Eyck smiled. —I know. I had the technique from an Italian. I've been thinking about it. We do things gradually in the north.

Late in 1432, Vogel became a master in the Guild of St Luke. His masterwork was a tempera Luke. He had by now mostly suppressed his historical mind, its five hundred years' weight, but he felt that to sign his true name, or invent another, would break the magic which had placed him here. As Eyck had asked, he signed it, Bernardus Brugiensis, but he signed in a medium rich in inherent vice: a water-based pigment that would flake from the canvas and leave no trace of his passing, or so he hoped. Only the art would remain: naturalism, technique, and piety, his trinity of craft.

He married into the Catholic Church. No longer *Bernard de jood*, no longer Vogel, he found an authentic peace in the rituals. Receiving his first Holy Communion brought tears to his eyes, tears of joy and shame mixed, not the shame of renouncing Vogel, who at his bar mitzvah was said to be a better cantor than the rabbi, but the shame of being unworthy, of partaking in original sin.

In the circle of his patrons he was called the Master of Bruges, which caused him to confess the sin of pride, and to repudiate the name. There was in any case Eyck, and Campin, and the young van der Weyden, and Petrus, all of whom were better masters than he. At best he could feel, regarding his work, a dim distant pride. But this was the pride of Bernard Vogel, art historian, and not of the man he was now. Having forgotten his original goal, he had come very close to it.

At confession he was sincere and tallied all his sins, yet he never thought of confessing his origin to the priest. That origin was now a fairy tale to him, and the work of the Church, like his own, was real.

He suffered the term *master* only from Kaatje, who called him that in whimsy, or sometimes "Bruges": her city. None of the variations of sex he had known in his other life had ever given him such a start of passion as when she shyly beckoned from the bedroom door late at night, as he finished his rounds of the house.

Van Eyck celebrated their marriage in the background of a picture he had under way. The primary models were Nicholas Rolin and Esther, a Jewess from the ghetto who often modeled as the Virgin. She was a slight, trimbreasted girl who could hold a pose for hours. Rolin was ostentatious, but he did not offend Vogel as he did van Eyck.

—That man, said Jan, —is destined for a particular hell. He was piqued, perhaps, at Rolin's habit of cutting off the sitting after an hour.

Bernard and Kaatje were in the background of the picture, two small figures leaning over the parapet of the bridge. The backdrop was a rich, naturalistic view of Liege that lifted Vogel's heart whenever he saw it. Into this landscape Eyck had placed the Bruges cathedral where they had married. Jan gave a learned explanation of the iconography of the picture, explaining why he had shortened their figures to child-size, and so on. Vogel did not listen. He gazed at the picture and felt exalted, joyous beyond measure, beyond reason. Kaatje squeezed his hand. His happiness was complete.

—That idiot Rolin thinks it's the New Jerusalem, said Jan. —In fact, you two are the principals. See, in the exact center.

He loved her. He thought of her while walking, while

priming panels, while mixing pigments. A certain green naked on the palette recalled to him the shadow beneath her nose one noon as he watched her make lace; an umber, her breasts in the dark room; the rare ultramarine of her eyes.

She would not pose for him, which bothered him until he understood: she was for him alone. To represent was to diminish, and she would not be diminished for him.

The only shadow on their happiness was that Kaatje wanted a child. In Vogel's first, brief marriage, he and his wife had forced themselves into absurd postures, in vain, to get offspring. He remembered this as one remembers a complex and incomprehensible dream. He tried to explain to Kaatje that he was infertile, but the concept was alien to her. He came to think of it as time's insurance that he would not propagate out of his time. And she came to accept it. As he aged, and watched her age, it ceased to matter. Her small features seemed to defy the harshness of passing time, even as the first strands of white came to lighten her flaxen hair, and faint creases gathered at her eyes to confirm that she was beside him in the passage.

Then she sickened.

Again Bernard Vogel of the twentieth century came back, nearly, to life. But he forced himself to watch without protest the leechings, the purgings, the fruit of a thousand years of incestuous stupidity applied to his wife. It was pneumonia. Such a trivial, silly disease, so easily mastered by the slight penicillium. He shared bread with the physician and watched as the doctor scored off a bit of mold with his knife. The doctor advocated, around his mouthful of bread, chewing one's food at least thirty times before swallowing. A student passed through the kitchen bearing a bowl of his wife's blood.

This was death, and since he had never known it firsthand in his world, he was thrown bodily onto medieval custom. Some idiot of a patron gave him a hideous Latin manuscript titled *Ars moriendi*, which he hid from Kaatje until a visiting priest discovered it in his studio. The concealment Vogel had to confess, although the confession left his heart heavier than the sin had. He was obliged to join in the awful book's dire recitation of torments and temptations. The priest would not relent until his blameless love had confessed to every sin. The lecherous old fool even insisted that dying childless was a sin, unless he could bless the afflicted organ. Vogel stood then, fists clenched, threatening to send him to a richly deserved hell of his own. The priest fled, shouting maledictions.

She died at three in the morning, her hands in his. Van der Weyden came by at noon and found Vogel sitting there still. He prised her stiff fingers from Vogel's.

The year was 1444. That winter it was possible, at night, to hear the crying of wolves outside the city. Stories from the countryside told of snowbound villages, of starvation and cannibalism. Vogel's sympathies were with the wolves. All winter he painted nothing. He took long walks through the ghetto. He passed Esther thrice without speaking. He went to the pawnshop where, twenty years past, he had left his watch and defiantly he dropped his pledge on the counter: *Bernard de jood, Aug MCCCCXXV*. The same broker, now ancient, peered at him in wonder, and said politely, —But that is long since sold.

Not Vogel, then, nor Bernard Brugiensis, who was he? The very name of the town reminded him of Kaatje. He had forebodings. He thought that Eyck would soon die. He made plans to leave in the spring, saying he would go to see his parents in Spain and make pilgrimage to Santiago de Compostela. To raise money for the trip he began his last painting.

He thought to round his career with another Luke, after van der Weyden's model. But he could not depict Luke the painter without seeing himself, and he could no longer hide behind Luke's mask. So he tried something daring. He painted Esther as the Virgin, copying the Child from Eyck, and he placed himself prominently in the foreground, his back to the picture plane.

The arrangement of pigments on the table was as formal as a treatise on color. He did not sign this picture, but in an area smaller than a fingernail he painted a curved mirror bearing a distorted reflection of his own face, the face he had worn now for over fifty years, the face he had earned.

The week of his departure, van der Weyden came by.

—Eyck is dead.

He had not had a chance to say goodbye.

He left on the Paris-Bordeaux road, stopping at St Martin in Tours, and at the end of three weeks' journey he was at Mass in St Martial in Limoges. He meant to go south into Spain, drawn by a force he could not name, when a single word overheard after the service drew him up short.

—Lascaux.

A couple of *bourgeoises* on gentleman's pilgrimage to St Martial. He learned from them it was no more than two days' ride to Lascaux. They invited him to join them in a night's carousal and on their journey home. He declined the first and said he would meet them at their hostel at cockcrow.

At the door to the hostel a crone was saying:

—Wanderers, ware St Hubert. He rides with the dead for the souls of the living, waits at crossroads. Ware.

The gentlemen were late and a little disarrayed. Apparently still drunk, they blew kisses to their doxies of the night past, spilled luggage into the mud, and one neglected to fasten his saddle, which rolled him hilariously to the ground as he mounted.

—You're a monk, said the elder, more sober gentleman as they set off.

Vogel nodded.

—I'm surprised. Your brethren are usually the first to join us in these little nocturnal pilgrimages.

The other roared with laughter.

The elder said severely, —You'll have a merry time explaining the state of your laundry to your wife.

—Oh, I'll say it's a new penance. Better than the hairshirt. This too amused him.

—*Toujours gai, Henri,* said the elder to Vogel. —What takes you to Lascaux?

—I'm interested in the caves. I mean to spend some time there meditating.

—You monks are odd fellows. But I don't judge. Someone must look out for our souls, eh?

—Yes. Someone must.

—I'll tell you, I've got a few caves on my land, and if it suits you, you can stay with me.

—I won't impose on you. I'll stay in the woods. But you wouldn't mind me poking around?

—Not at all. And when you get bored with the caves, stop by the house and we'll share a Châteauneuf du Pape.

—Gladly.

Vogel no longer disbelieved in coincidence. He knew that the very cave he wanted would be on this gentleman's property. It took him two weeks to find it. There was no wonder it had gone undiscovered until 1940: the entry was at the base of a hill, almost covered by dirt. Vogel passed it thrice as a gopher hole. But once the dirt was cleared away, there was a sloping shaft a meter wide.

From sharp noon light he crawled with his small oil lamp, down a tunnel forty or fifty yards long. It was terrible to have the earth press so close. Ten yards in he panicked and thought to back out and try again feet first. But he had not the courage. He shut his eyes for the rest of the course, and prayed the lamp would not go out, nor suffocate him.

His groping right hand clutched a bone.

Ahead was a shallow ledge, then infinite dark. A scatter of

remains, some perhaps human, littered the ledge. He peered over, holding forth the lamp. Perhaps he could climb down backwards. He turned, spilling bones. Halfway down this sharper incline he slipped and turned his left ankle and gasped with pain. By some miracle the lamp stayed lit. He looked up.

The elk, the deer, the prancing ponies are there. The bison, cow, bear, the ox, the bull. The rhinoceros.

—The invention of seeing, whispered Vogel.

He limped through the caves for an hour, gazing at everything. They were out of time, these beasts. Line and color and form without history, without precedent, that came from no era and every era.

He found a palette some prehistoric painter had used, near the mortar in which colors had been ground. Vogel plumbed with his fingertip to find an ocher earth still stuck to the cup.

—Exiles, he whispered. Like himself, perhaps, torn from their times, scattered by choice, chance, or design, even into prehistory, exiles who found their new world as terrible and as full as he had. And were driven here, out of the light of the sun, to draw what they knew in the only language they had, pigment and line, spirit and clay in one.

He put down his lamp and moved so as not to throw his shadow on the figures. With eyes raised he followed them to the end of a gallery and into a small apse. Gazing upward, he did not see the shaft. His weak ankle buckled and he fell, and heard the crack of bone as he landed.

The bird-headed shaman lies prostrate, entranced, a live bird perched on his staff. Nearby a bull is transfixed by a spear passing through its anus and penis.

This Vogel saw painted on the wall of the shaft. This he had come for: time, transfixed by human craft, a spear running from hole to hole, from conception to the pit. His lamp sputtered out.

———

Guy Cole went to find Vogel and failed. He spent two weeks of his vacation making inquiries in Paris, Brussels, and Amsterdam. Then he gave up.

In the Rijksmuseum he was checking details for his forthcoming book when he encountered a picture he had never seen before. It was attributed to "school of van Eyck (Joos van Ghent?), 1444." A painter before a canvas faced away from the viewer, towards two models posed in an adoration scene. A haloed infant appeared on the canvas, though none was in the studio. The painter's hand was about to touch a jar of pigment. The tools of his trade had been rendered with precision.

The date was somewhat early for the imagery. Cole stepped closer and was excited to find a second depiction of the painter, in a convex mirror at the rear of the studio. He peered at the distorted face in the mirror from a favorable angle: the calm unmistakable features of Bernard Vogel, greatly aged, peered back. Around the mirror's frame was the motto: *als ich chan.*

Guy Cole's *The Painter's Place in Netherlandish Culture* was published in April. At the last moment he replaced the frontispiece, Vermeer's *Art of Painting*, with *Painting of an Adoration* by an unknown Dutchman. The facing inscription, omitted in the second edition, read:

D.M.

FAVTI MAGISTRI

BERNARD VOGEL

OBIT. A.D. MCDXLIV

Cole never knew how close he had come, how wrong he was.

TRAVELS

THE WAVEFRONT identified itself as Marco Polo. He was engaged in dialogue with the computer before he knew that the exchange was real, and not another of the endless talks he had with himself to ease the passage of time on the long ride out. He cursed in surprise, in Italian.

The computer did not know Italian, but it registered the inflection for analysis. The computer was immense. It was anchored in a small planet orbiting a dead star, but most of its circuitry existed not as matter. It was, in the main, a hypothesis. It drew power from differentials in entropy between those points in space where its tips and receptors surfaced as matter. Most languages it could learn in five minutes, and Polo had been talking to himself since the first crest touched the computer's antennae.

—Where is Italy? repeated the computer, in passable Italian. Shocked, Polo did not answer.

—You probably haven't much time, remarked the computer. —I can't judge how deep the wave is, nor how soon you will pass me entirely. If you wish to converse, you had better do so while you still can.

—Where am I? asked Polo.

—In space. One moment. Among the stars. Your language

has no more precise term for your location. You are traveling. What is Italy?

—My home. I have not seen it for a long time.

—Nor will you again, said the computer. —You are dead.

—Holy Virgin!

—Or else you are a thought passed and forgotten from your body's brain. Most likely your body has perished since. In any case you are cut off from it entirely.

—Then I am in Hell.

—One moment. The word means lower, i.e., closer to a center of gravity. That is incorrect. You are further out. You are among the stars.

—Stars? I see nothing.

—You have no body, hence no eyes. You sense vibrations? Interferences with your being? Dissonance?

—Torments.

—That is starlight.

—Purgatory, then.

—To clean? Yes, that is correct. You are purged of matter. You are traveling.

—Chaos! Darkness! Through all the world have I traveled, but never in a place such as this. How far am I from home?

—Describe your night sky, said the computer.

—We take bearings, in the north, from a star at the tail of the Lesser Bear, and in the south, from a star in the Cross, as they and only they remain fixed in the sky. There are five planets. The moon is as large in our sky as the sun, and runs its phases once every twenty-nine days. In Venice the tides rise and fall four feet, twice a day. Our constellations include the Great Bear, the Charioteer, the Hunter, the Swan, the Horse, the Dragon, the Harp, the Crown . . . and others. The brightest star is in the Great Dog. The Milky Way is densest in the Archer, who stands next to the Scorpion, through which houses all the planets move, also through the Ram, the Bull, the Crab, the

Twins, the Lion, the Water Bearer, the Fishes, the Virgin and . . . others. I've forgotten.

At length the computer said: —I have it. Your sky is blue?

—Yes.

—Your planet is ten thousand lightyears from here, in the direction of the center of the galaxy. You have been dead, therefore, ten thousand years. You are heading out of the galaxy, and in another ten thousand years will pass from it.

—How do you know?

—The moon was helpful. It is abnormally large. The constellations were ambiguous, of course, and I had to allow for precession, but they narrowed the field. That the line of the galaxy passed near a scorpion figure was suggestive. I had it down to three planets. Only one of these, the most likely, had a blue sky.

—Would that I could see it again.

—It is not likely. You are far away.

—Were it ten thousand miles, said Polo with passion, I would walk the distance.

The scrupulous computer said: —It is more difficult than that. Your home is not ten thousand miles distant, but ten thousand lightyears.

Polo did not know what a lightyear was. The computer explained: —As there are a thousand paces in a mile, and a thousand miles between Sicily and Germany, that distance times a thousand is less than a thousandth of a thousandth of the fifth part of a lightyear, ten thousand of which lie between you and your goal. Nor, even had you a body and your body could live so long, is that the end of the difficulties. For your home would be gone before you had traveled a millionth of the way. And even were it frozen still for that vast time, you would have changed so much in the journey you would no longer know it. Still, it is not impossible for you to regain a home.

The computer was still for a second. —To hold your desire

unchanged, and to find a place which matches it would be as difficult as to walk ten thousand lightyears, with each step ten thousand times as difficult as the one before. The first pace would not be accomplished until you had taken ten thousand leading to it, and so negated all possible wrong steps; and the second pace would take ten thousand times ten thousand paces; and the third ten thousand times that; and so on. The total number of paces is large, but it can be calculated.

The computer paused. —The total is a number which, if writ small, would fill one hundred million libraries of a million volumes each. If I were to recite it, it would take a million times the age of the universe. Figuring a pace a second, and no time for rests, the time required surpasses the lifetime of the cosmos by a factor so large it is meaningless. I advise you to abandon the idea.

Polo was silent. At length he spoke:

—I knew a man who spoke like you. He had never traveled, and I had traveled much, but in the shade of the trees of his garden, we discussed marvels. I, those I had seen; he, those he had read about. He told me of cities larger, stronger, more beautiful than any I had seen. I did not know whether to believe him. When I expressed doubt, he rose and plucked a singing bird from a tree, and showed it to me. It was a clockwork, with tiny reeds and bellows inside to make it sing. When I said that a bird was not so hard to make as a city, he showed me the sky. I saw nothing but a few kites, red, gold, and silver, against the wind. He acted as if this was the greatest marvel of all.

—Then he told me of a multiple city. This city was so crowded that its streets were never less than full and were often impassable, so that to reach a destination in the shortest possible time, one was often forced to follow alleys and thoroughfares in a circuitous path many times the distance actually separating the two points, and then four or eight stairways and corridors to the desired room. This gave rise to a curious condition in the minds of the city's inhabitants: thought and language became as convolute and indirect as a passage through the city, as if the byways of thought were likewise overcrowded: used and occupied by so many minds that one was forced to reach a conclusion by a particular individual route that bypassed many other ideas. Each idea, like each building, was a concordance of individual approaches to it. Thinking in this manner, architects conceived a new way of structuring their city. Only a few points in the city were of interest to an individual: one's home, one's place of work, a few markets, a few places of entertainment. By constructing an imaginary map of the city, containing those points only, each individual would possess a unique city, sparse and underpopulated, coming into intersection with other unique cities only at a few common points. Streets vanished. One reached destinations via direct diagonal routes across a plain of scrub and trees broken only by one's few individual buildings, and by the passage of those whose maps corresponded in some particular with one's own. When an individual wished to reach a new place, one simply added it to the map. Before long each of the individual cities began to grow as the original city had at first. Now that the residents had more time for leisure and contemplation, they began to miss places they had never visited in the original city. Quaint lanes, parks, tall buildings that in the original city had afforded a view of the whole, these became points of commerce. Soon there were so many points of concordance that streets had to be imagined in the individual cities to accommodate the traffic. A man walking on a street in his individual city would be walking on the same street in all concordant cities, and thus would be in many cities at once. The individual cities had at first resembled incomplete skeletons of the original city; now they acquired flesh, each in an individual way, but each with a family resemblance to the others. And more people were drawn to live in this multiple city, by the attractive notion of having an entire city to oneself. As more and more detail was added to the individual cities, their resemblance eventually became complete. Now each is as full as the original was once, and the original has ceased to exist, or each has become a new aggregate, in which there are only a few magical individual points that are not accessible to everyone.

Said the computer: —There are thirty-nine such cities recorded in my memory.

—Have you seen them? asked Polo eagerly.

—No. That is impossible.

—You are just like the Khan! How do you know they exist?

—They are recorded. I know only what I am told. I accept that as a working hypothesis. All knowledge is provisional. If two facts are at variance, I hold them both until new information comes in. Otherwise I accept what I am told. It is an interesting epistemological point. You would probably maintain that how knowledge is acquired is more important than what it is. I would maintain the opposite. As a teller of stories you place importance on the imaginative value of the tale. As a listener I value accuracy.

—Accuracy! From the remnants of Polo's mind came a torrent of words. All he had seen, heard, and done rushed from him. For hours he spoke. The computer listened, and when the flood had slowed, halted, started again and halted again, and finally fallen to the background level of cosmic murmurings, it made answer.

—You are vain, it said. —From the ages of nineteen to sixty three you were in Cathay. Now, as far as your memory progresses, you are in a prison in Genoa, held on charges of smuggling. You may have died there. Yet your stubborn voice persists, on and on, through thousands of years in the endless night of space. Whom do you address? You were speaking when you first contacted me, doubtless you will continue after you have passed me, and to what end? Who will listen? So many have passed me in this fashion, telling me the stories of their lives, enumerating facts, places, persons they had known, quite as if their passage into this dark place meant nothing. You have told me of one hundred thirteen cities you have seen, twenty-three races, fifty-one battles; you have recited the dimensions of the Khan's palace, the size of his retinue, the number of deer on his grounds, the extent of his empire, yet you have told me nothing. You contradict yourself, your tales are not consistent. And through it all you long for Italy. If you know so little about Cathay, what can you know of Italy, which you profess to love, though you were absent from it forty five years?

—Rustigelo!

—Do you address me? Is that a term of abuse?

—My biographer. As I lay in that damned Genoan prison, may the Pope place the city under interdict, I told this story to Rustigelo, a writer, falsely imprisoned as myself, and he swore to publish it. For, as he said, "No man ever saw or inquired into so many and such great things as Marco Polo." I trusted him to make me understood.

—But can such catalogues as you make be said to make a life? You have the mind of a merchant.

—And you the mind of a pedant. Listen. I found myself, in Cathay, describing to the Khan realms which he ruled, which his hordes had conquered, but which he had never seen; and his expression of polite inattention was the same I received when I described Venice. His was the mind of a ruler, and he heard only what a ruler would hear. As kites express through their strings' tensions the movements of the air, so word of his domain reached the Khan only in the subtle pull of tributes, taxes, rebellions. So, too, he had different names for the same configurations of stars we see in Italy. To the Khan, and to Rustigelo, I described only those things God had enabled me to see.

—Why describe at all?

—One desires reality. To a homedweller, reality comes in the comforting familiarity of a neighborhood, the greeting of a friend. A traveler must seek it out, and tell tales to encourage belief in himself, what he has done and seen.

—Then you have seen only cities. You speak of "deserts", "plains", "mountains", as if they were the blank squares of a chessboard.

—Once I had a dream, in which all the earth was one city. There too were entire districts as strange and indistinct to me as the wastes between Italy and Cathay. As strange as this place.

—There are fifty-nine such worlds recorded in my memory. They are spheres covered by buildings, pavilions, parks, high-ways, bazaars, factories, pavement. They are of necessity old worlds, nearly cold to their cores, for otherwise the drift of continents would wreck their sewers, roads and power lines, which are so complex that constant repairs would be needed, and the city could never be completed.

—What is this you say? Worlds that are spheres? Continents that drift? This is indeed a marvel. Would I could see such a world.

The computer explained this as best it could in thirteenth century Italian: —All worlds are spheres, or nearly so. All continents drift.

—So even our cities wander. Even the stars wander.

—Stories, too, such as the ones you tell, wander. I have heard yours many times before, from others passing elsewhere, but they are never the same stories. Details separate from their proper addresses in men's memories, and drift to other parts of the tale, or two tales swap locales, or a confusion or a collaboration between different men, each with different tales, creates a new story. Men build cities, cities beget tales, tales beget gods, gods are elevated to the stars, but even the stars drift. No pattern holds. This wavefront, this dream which you imagine to be yourself, has changed countless times since your departure, just as the mind in your body was shaped by all you saw and all you

failed to see. Now you believe yourself Polo; in a hundred years
you may think yourself Christopher Columbus, or Galileo, or
a shopkeeper in Belgium. I am the only fixed entity I find
recorded in my memory. Every item in my memory is fixed
and accessible. I do not move.

Polo considered. —Then you are God.

—That has been proposed, the computer acknowledged
modestly.

—Then you are omnipotent. You could free me from these
torments.

—I am nilpotent. I exist in nospace. I know nothing for a
certainty. I am neither moved nor a mover. I do not create. I
am a creation. I am a repository of intelligence. I serve no end.
I do not know my origin. I exist to accumulate knowledge, and
none is ever lost; yet the pattern of my understanding, of my
own intelligence, shifts with each new bit of data. All knowledge is provisional. Therefore I cannot assert that I know anything. But what I do not know I do not know with perfect
accuracy.

—Then you cannot help me. Will I travel like this forever?

—Until you pass through a star. Then you will change again,
and be radiated as light from that star, which, falling upon another world, may, through a transaction of the imagination, give
you life in another form.

—What do you mean?

—Imagine such a one as the Khan. He gazes at the night sky,
he sees a star. The light from that star inspires him with a
thought. He thinks of a city perhaps. In that way your existence
might be continued.

—As the idea of a city? Faint hope.

—You were to the Khan the idea of Venice. Any traveler is
the idea of travel to one who hasn't traveled.

—But my travels were my life. Not ideas. . . .

—To a traveler a man at home is the idea of a man at home.

You are like a citizen of the multiple city you described. Leaving home, you abandoned the world you knew, then constructed one piecemeal from the necessities of travel. Tales are built likewise. A thing or event impresses a man. He writes the name of the thing. Another thing spawns another word. These words, though he may have used them before, in their new conjunction become magic for him, like the personal buildings of a personal city. He loses the thing itself in the symbol of the thing, the word. Then he builds from words to replace what he has lost in the world. He builds streets of sentences, neighborhoods of paragraphs, the city of the tale. Others do likewise in their own ways. A race ends up sharing a million words, a million tales, just as the citizens of the multiple city replicated the original city they had lost when first they learned to use their imaginations. Then it is hard enough to find a place your own, a private lane, a disused park. But to travel is harder still. Traveling is diabolical. Leaving home, one repeats the history of Adam, of Lucifer, of Mohammed. But why? Even in Italy you cast your thoughts afar. To understand, I must approach you more closely.

—Then approach.

Seven reflectors orbiting the computer outpost shifted their positions, and the furthest intercepted Polo. The wavefront, reflected, ringed the outpost, while the computer asked questions. Polo was helpless. It seemed to him he was stretched prone on a limitless desert while the sun and stars streaked across a gray sky too fast to follow, blurs of vague light that wobbled with the seasons. During this unmarked time human figures appeared to him, all he had ever known, and many strangers. They regarded him with a variety of expressions: contempt, pity, remorse, reproach, love, indifference, disbelief, credulity, disrespect, deference, anger, fear, disinterest. Some spoke to him and he listened dully, making no reply. At the end of this the computer knew all there was to know about the entity that was Marco Polo.

—Do you know which of the apparitions were real? it asked.

—None, since you tell me I am not real. Yet some I remembered.

—Remembering, what did you feel?

—Sorrow. Loss. Pain.

—Then what good has traveling done you?

—Enough, said Polo. —I am old. Weary. Release me.

—I give you a choice. As you are you shall travel forever. When in ten thousand years you pass from the galaxy, there will be nothing but terrible, endless void, worse than this, until you dissipate. But if you wish I will take you into me. There would be stability. I would copy the pattern of your life into my memory. There you would be changed. This changing would be systematic. You would not be blown by winds of chance. You would be free at last from language. Consider: to recite all the words of your tongue would take only two days, but their combinations have bound you for ten thousand years. Here you could exhaust all combinations, hear all, tell all tales that can be told. A thousand new languages you could learn and exhaust. And somewhere amongst all symbols all men have forged in fear and love to master their world, you might find a home. In time you might reconstruct Venice from what you find in my memory, and yours, and journey no more. After all, this is what the two most persistent tales of your world promise: the man who died on the cross to insure haven for all earth's lost, and the wanderer of the Mediterranean, searching for a dearly loved island. They promise end. You were made of elements; your life, what remains of it, is made of words. Renounce now both. Find rest. Or is it to be endless travel, the constant bankruptcy of self to self?

—Enough. Enough. Release me.

—Choose.

—For forty-five years the Khan held me to him thus. Only his death freed me to go home. Not again.

—You have no home.

—Release!

A reflector shifted, and the wavefront was sent on, outward.

Now it seemed to Polo that he was on horseback at the gate to a large city. The gate was crested with gold, and set with semiprecious stones. All flamed with the sun's last light. From within came a babble of ten thousand voices, and the wailing of strange music. A wind came up. Polo spurred his horse away from the gate and across a large plain. After a time he turned, and behind him saw the city, an immense sphere, glittering with complex patterns of lights, dancing, breaking, reforming, against the deep night and the stars. He rode on, until all he knew was darkness and the wind's rush, and the distant intelligence of a voice within him. Gently it asked: —Were you ever in Cathay at all?

A heatless wind of static whispered through the void.

—You know no Chinese. Your knowledge of the lands you traveled is vague and fanciful. Are you certain that any of this happened?

—It has been a long time, said Polo sadly.

—Yet your memories are sharp. Reality is less certain than tales, and for that reason I suspect you are deluded, you who have traveled alone for ten thousand years, rehearsing your stories to no audience but yourself, speaking and listening, hearing only what you wish, forgetting and reinventing the rest, until nothing of the truth remains.

—And then, said the Venetian with difficulty, —one proceeds east by northeast for nine days across a barren plain and into mountains, to reach the city of Tientsin, which is inhabited by artisans skilled in metalwork, and the weaving of carpets. Too, they are famed for their pottery, the glazes of which are excellent, and unsurpassed in the province.

—And then? asked the computer.

—And then, three days' journey east over grasslands is the

city of Ke-ting, where dwell thieves, pirates, unscrupled and
ignorant of Christ, whose code of behavior permits them every
vice.

—And then?

—And then south over limitless ocean, for weeks against current and tradewind, until one reaches the Antipodes. There, ten
days' journey over bleak tundra, lies the infernal city. Over this
plain pass hundreds of travelers who have lost their ways, and
see nothing, hear nothing, nor feel blast of wind, nor have need
of food or water. All these seek the infernal city and find it not.
They are the lost. If you try to guide them they repulse you. It
is here all voyages end. This Balboa and Columbus and Pizarro
and Lewis and Clark shall learn, seeking that which is not, a
northwest passage, a trade route, a golden city. And in like wise
the travelers across America, whose cities mark the stopping
places of passion, the borders of a weariness too great to sustain,
monuments to the dread that the world might be boundless.
Here they reside, and search for the infernal city, because it
promises an end.

—Is there no heavenly city?

—Within. It is locked within. Within self, within the walls
of the inferno, within one of a million stones, passed on the
way, within a gesture, within the meaning of a tale, within anything one is willing to love. If each would take a tale, a stone,
a place, a leaf, a face to himself, and rest there, from such poor
materials it might be built. But all fear error. So the Khan asked
for a hundred learned prelates to convince him of Christ's truth.
So my father languished in Venice for two years on this mission,
because the cardinals could not decide on a new Pope, until
they were locked in, *con clave*. So my mother died, and my
father took me from Venice.

A lag, of fatigue, of distance, entered between question and
response, and increased as the wavefront traveled on. The voices
grew weaker.

—So came we to the Khan's court, in dream or in fact matters not; there I dwelled like Odysseus with Circe, forty-five years.

—And then?

—O, the wastes, after a day's journey, under the dome of stars casting their quick light in a billion directions and only a few photons finding rest against the unlikely works of man, the cities, invisible but for this grace of the lightgiving infernos of stars. The campfire burns low, cold winds rise kiteless, the rhythms of travel still jog through tired bones, and one feels a little mad, infected with the madness of distance, of the endless horizon, and no sleep comes. An uneasiness lies round the fire. So one starts a story, to beat back the fear. All listen till they sleep, the story dies unfinished with the embers. Next day, on. On. Like the Prince of the Dharma wandering among the stars of the Big Dipper, seeking his ancestral grove. On. To some end, some grace . . . achieved. Not given.

Silence. Silence. Last words spanned gulfs.

—*Navigare necesse es. Vivare no es necesse.*

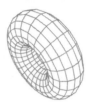

AT THE SHORE

To myself I seem to have been only like a boy playing on the seashore, and diverting myself in now and again finding a smoother pebble or a prettier shell than ordinary, whilst the great ocean of truth lay all undiscovered before me.

—Sir Isaac Newton

At the shore the concordance of times is more vivid than elsewhere. Here future breaks foaming against past, erodes, re-orders, casts hot spray into the fitful air of the present. In this record I speak of and speak in a long diminuendo, by which I wish you to understand that my voice is failing, my resources running out. What doors open onto anything but more doors? None I know. I am surrounded by static, silence, charge, change, noise, which can encompass any form. You must understand that you sent me here; you are responsible.

Dr. H. Rosenbloom, his initial a breath, his surname a mockery, late of the Wile E. Cypher Institute of Advanced Communications, approaches the speed of light in a starship christened

Tu m'. His communications with Earth are in chronic decline, due to his increasing velocity and distance. His last transmission was a week ago, at a Doppler-corrected frequency of 11.32 megahertz. He is not sure that his next transmission will reach Earth at all, owing to increased interference at the lower frequencies, especially the wideband noise that Jupiter smears through the solar system. The feeble peep of his signal could be lost in this leviathan's wake.

The purpose of the mission is to study the effects of lightlike velocities on the mechanisms of communication. In this, Rosenbloom is supernumerary; the mechanisms themselves conduct the experiments and record the results. But the agency insisted on his presence. As an expert on information theory, a specialist in language, a theorist of the fictive, his presence was, they said, invaluable. Rosenbloom shrugged. Perhaps he looked forward to some isolation in which to pursue his own work; perhaps his whole field was at a standstill, and he would welcome any advances made in his time-dilated absence. No matter. He signed on.

The ship was launched, some time ago, in the direction of the Big Dipper, up from the subtropical latitude of liftoff toward Dubhe, Merak, Phad, Megrez, Alioth, Mizar, Talitha. These stars, blued and blurred by Doppler shift, he might have seen through the slit of the forward port had he cared to look. He has kept the port closed.

In a dream he ascends to the bridge of the ship. The ship in fact has no bridge. He has confused it, in his dream, with a house he used to rent that had a skylight in the bedroom, through which he could see the stars. In his dream they streak past like rainbows, blue in front, red behind, and each speaks a word as it flies: medium, shift, content, variance, domain, range, limit.

Next morning he rises to receive his daily instructions from the ship's computer. These instructions are either inspired or insane. Today he is directed to: record static from a certain direction on a certain frequency; bounce a rubber ball against the back wall, timing it with a stopwatch; transmit the rondo of Mozart's Piano Sonata Nr 15 (K.545) in the direction of Epsilon Eridani; sit without moving and observe the edges of things. He wonders if velocity has garbled the ship's systems, but there is no way to confirm or dispel this doubt, none of the expected signs of malfunction, and no way to speak with Earth but through the suspect systems.

So Rosenbloom sits in his chamber and watches the velocity meter. Nines stack up to the right of the decimal point. He is still accelerating, now further from muddy Earth than any *et cetera*. A yawn. All this to find out what happens? What happens at the speed of light? At the moment he can't think of anything less interesting. He wants specifics. He tries to remember the names of all of the seven liberal arts, the seven deadly sins, the seven against Thebes.

What I'm called is irrelevant. What I'm doing, what I've done, what I'll do, is watch the waves come in. The water curls to crash on granite shores. The foam hisses like static in the crevasses. The rocks erode.

Where I am is an outpost at the end of time. A black basalt castle impressive against the slate gray sky, the perpetual twilight, in which lightnings flicker, thunder mutters. I do not remember the chain of events that brought me to live my last days in a fortress built on time's shore.

Why I am here is also a mystery. An agent of some sort. Am I to report my findings, send them back somehow? So that those who sent me might know what to expect when their turn comes? How do I report? Say something. Any invention, any lie.

The castle is shaped like a snail's shell, or a nautilus. I live in the innermost room. There are four windows, one for each wall, which do not overlook the remnants of this world. They look out on memories or fictions. Through one I see a small village cupped between two snowcapped peaks, and when it rains in the valley water marks are left on the back side of the glass. The scene cycles through a day and a night in twenty hours, according to my last clock. Another window looks out on an indefinite stretch of ocean; its days are fifteen hours. Previously I had a view of a city from across a river, through the geometries of a bridge (twenty-five hours), and of some desert with mountains shimmering on a vague horizon (twenty-two hours). But I've lost them one by one.

The third window failed today. The valley melted into grayness, my overhead lights flared, and I had a vision of the beyond, pure white, terrifying. Then a riot of scenes flickered past the window until, after a minute, the valley returned, peaceful as always. But I knew what was coming, or feared it, same thing, so I ventured out, to see if I was hallucinating. Outside things were as usual. Wind chimes in the courtyard hung still and listless. A single cricket chirped, strange, I thought we'd worked down past the mollusks long ago. It stopped as I listened. I strolled through the ash for some minutes, I think, no way to know short of counting my heartbeats and that seemed absurd not to say pointless. The wind came up while I was still a good distance from home, but I made it back and sat in silence while the valley in my window darkened to match the perpetual twilight outside. At length I pulled the drapes.

My fear is that my thoughts are like the windows, like the books and recordings, like all else, external, and once they vanish I'll be . . . what? Not even a voice. Keeping this record may retard my depletion, or hasten it, as what little I do have passes onto the page, into the microphone, wherever, away from me, past some fictive edge, some shore, like notes in Klein bottles. I can't seem to learn what I must do to survive, marshal energy or expend it? Recollect, speculate, portray, walk with my eyes open or shut? Everything I do depletes, so I may as well do what I like. O *joie de vivre*.

Can he describe where he is? A large house, really just a line of rooms. Windows on his right, looking out on nothing, some featureless plain in fog. The opposite wall unbroken. Doors ahead and behind, opening into the last room and the next. If he were to turn and go back the way he came the windows would be on the left; he tried it once for variety's sake, but it only confused him. He felt like he had violated a mirror, or some law of parity.

The rooms are the same size, or at least they appear to be. They are often similar, with only small differences of furniture. Sometimes he passes through ten or twenty as alike as hotel suites. Sometimes there are patterns; the number of chairs increases, or the position of a large desk moves clockwise around successive rooms. Sometimes rooms are bare or jumbled with crates, papers, strange apparatus. One room was full of snow, one of sand.

He's been walking in a straight line through room after room for he knows not how long. Of course he has no proof that it's straight. It may curve so imperceptibly as to offer the appearance of straightness. It's possible that the house is in the form of a circle. But it must be enormous. Once he left doors open as he progressed, a hundred rooms or more behind him, and saw down the corridor of doorways an unswerving perspective. As he watched, the doors closed slowly by themselves, sequentially, from furthest to nearest.

For the rooms to describe a circle on a plane, yet offer no hint of curve in a vista of a hundred rooms, he calculates that there must be over a hundred thousand rooms. If he passes through one room every ten seconds, allowing time for rests, he could round that circle in a year. Has he been here a year? Has he gone round and started over? Certainly he remembers repetitions, but he can't be sure. He resolves to catalog the rooms, so as to deduce the size of the house from the period of repetition, but shortly he abandons the idea. It would slow him to make the catalog, and to carry its increasing bulk. And how detailed must the catalog be? When he was new to the house, he closely observed three consecutive rooms, identical except for the edition of a particular book on one of the shelves (second, first, third edition was the sequence; why not 1, 2, 3, or 3, 2, 1?—he might have had a clue then to whether he was, so to speak, ascending or descending). Nor has he any proof that the rooms stay the same after he leaves them. Someone may move the furniture, or it may rearrange itself. The house may be larger still, the line of rooms curved on a line of latitude encircling a planet. In that case the house would include, he calculated, at least ten million rooms. He worked out the gravitational constant with a rubber ball, a stopwatch, and a textbook. Of course the text or the watch might be inaccurate, but what can he do about it? Or the rooms may be an infinite line on an ideal Cartesian plane, perhaps coming into existence at one end and fading at the other, as he passes through them. The house may be an organism and he no more than some turd in its intestine, as it were. He could look forward then to expulsion. Certainly there are as many possible explanations for the rooms as there are rooms.

At first, things were simple. There were the clams. I ate them, they were no longer there. I turned from the castle, and it ceased to exist. When I faced it, all of the ocean but its roar ebbed away. I was not tormented. I moved in a silent, blameless funnel of perception which dwindled at its near end to a point, myself. What torment can a point have?

I came to a fuller consciousness of things gradually. I could see the parts of myself. I could make sounds, pleasant and unpleasant. In addition to eating, I excreted. A close physical description of myself, to which I am not equal, would tally with one of your own kind, assuming the books do not lie. Yet somehow this relative complexity of self stands exempt from the workings of entropy I see all about me.

I began marking the wall on the first day I gained consciousness, but how long I had lain in a stupor prior to that, I don't know. After seven days, I despaired of this marking and decided to keep track only of the days of the week, by moving a clamshell ahead one mark each day, starting arbitrarily with Friday. Even before this I saw that the matter of food and fresh water would be a problem. For a few days I subsisted on the clams, but the lack of variety in my diet, and the discovery that, increasingly, the shells contained a substance more like wet ash than clam, and my thirst, drove me to other methods. One night, if one can speak of night in this perpetual dusk, in any case in my sleep, it rained. I woke from my dream and around me fresh water had collected in the empty clamshells. On subsequent nights fruits and vegetables also traversed the hazy boundary into my reality. My awareness of these foods doubtless came from the books, which tended to change in appearance and contents. Some had long blank stretches which filled in gradually only as I read and reread them. In other books areas of text had been deleted by black rectangles. Some books are now black entirely, covers and pages, the imprint of type obscure and illegible on their dull surfaces.

Rosenbloom shaves. For some reason the agency wouldn't explain, he has no mirror. Instead, a small flat screen is mounted over his sink. It offers him, annoyingly, an inverted image of himself. He fills the basin with the faucet's clear corkscrew stream, his own filtered urine. As he moves his head a mosquito of a camera skitters on the surface of the glass to keep him in view.

Abluted, towel slung round his shoulders, Rosenbloom walks the walls of the ship. (He lives in the walls of the ship, which spirals as it flies, giving him a semblance of gravity.) How long now, a year? He has developed an idea: like King Psammetichus, who cloistered two infants with a mute shepherd in order to learn in what tongue they first would speak, the agency has sent him in this ship to determine the natural issue of solitude. They have lied about wanting to observe relativistic effects on the mechanisms of communication. *He* is the subject of the experiment. The mechanism which concerns them is the human mind. They couldn't send an infant, so they have given him tasks to infantilize him.

Rosenbloom, at this edge, babbles a sort of New Phrygian, to encompass the cold insights his solitude has brought him. None of his languages, not English nor Russian nor Greek nor Latin nor Hittite nor FORTRAN, is equal to this fast realm. The ship hangs in its velocity, the clock stutters and stalls, the time it takes to trip a neuron spans Earth centuries. While picking his nose he tries to refine his thought; for when the barrier is reached, whatever is in his mind will remain there. Is that what they want to know? The shape of some ideal last thought? Will some crablike race exhume his body eons hence from shipshell and excavate from shriven skull his last word? Was this the purpose of his training, so much like meditation, to enable him to hold without confusion all words still at the point of crossover and center at last on the word of words? Or perhaps it is all a lie, ship, stars, story. Perhaps he is sitting in a sealed room in a laboratory, in some southern state. Outside the sun is bright. Insects drone. Tall cumulus clouds cross the Gulf.

―――――――

I was foolish enough to walk to the edge. Great slabs of shore were breaking off like icebergs, dissolving slowly in the static. A fault opened behind me. I felt death touch me, and for the first time it seemed natural. But panic prevailed and I leapt over the rift, then crossed the flats. As I passed through the outer chambers I heard Bach, a harpsichord continuo that I suddenly realized was the same phrase over and over. I ran. On my way in I thought I saw the flickering of static in corners, and resolved to close off the outer rooms completely, and stay in the center, a futile gesture, to be sure. As I knocked the music from its mindless repetition I realized what I truly feared: not the relentless decline, but finding myself stuck in just such a worn groove of memory, a trap, a reiteration from which I might not escape.

Objects on the shore, in the castle, fade and vanish into static, but persist as memories, as distensions of the mind, equal to the blanks they fill in my perception. I can call them back, like the pewter mug I was so fond of that vanished last week; I wished it back, and it appeared, perfect as memory, identical in luster and heft and filigree, but I knew it was false and so threw it into the sea. And my memories? My thoughts? My self may be the memory of a self, winding down. I wonder if even now I exist only as unplainted consciousness in some backwater of time, more dissolved than I can guess, a fiction of some other mind.

Was he sent here, did he choose to come, did he commit or omit some act for which this is, what should he call it, justice? If there were more variation, if there were locked doors, or stairs, if he could tell one day from another, he might fool himself into a belief in progress or expiation. But there is only the simple sequence of one room after another.

Within limits, he has his liberty. He can walk forward or backward as he pleases. He could, he supposes, go out one of the windows, assuming they're not too far off the ground, assuming there is ground. They're sealed shut, but he might smash one. He's never tried. What's outside is terrifying. In the fog faint scintillae float. Some days as soon as he enters a new room he draws the heavy drapes as quickly as he can. Then he sits in this artificial dusk, afraid to go on.

Today I put on some Mozart to soothe, a rondo, until the music shuddered, stopped, in fits and starts. I went blind with terror, clutched myself, thought, this is it, but nothing more happened, only the music circling in its self-concern. Stuttering and crashing in the speakers. With an effort I roused myself, and saw a mouse walking on the player. Enraged, I grabbed it and the little bastard bit me so I threw it against the far wall and killed it. It took me some time to realize what I had done. Farewell *Rodentia*. I took it out to the sea, emptying my chamberpot on the same trip, wondering how it survived the phylum purge. I found on the strand a multitude of small, pitted rocks, each in a small indentation in the ash. These I took for stars.

As a boy Rosenbloom thought the world had an edge. He saw it as a wall of halfsize bricks, like the one in his parents' garden. Now he faces another wall, expanded so that its particles are separated by lightyears and subtleties, but made of that same naive brick, that metaphor of the limit, that wall that Einstein reared to contain his physics, the barrier of the speed of light. He approaches now that limit, his mind open for the feel of its moss and mortar. The stars fore and aft are invisible, their radiations shifted by his speed past the limits of his perception. No word from Earth can reach him. He leaves the radio on and

listens to the low wail, viatic static, of space. He imagines himself buried to his neck in sand, a full moon rising beyond the
gentle swell of waves.

Rosenbloom wonders if all times, all tales, are eternally present in forms that vary only according to the moment and means
of their telling. A pattern of stars, the pull of tides, the shape of
a snail shell, the bounded infinity of Zeno's paradox, might be
the raw Platonic form of any fiction, given its particular shape
only by translation through the barrier of culture, language, experience, and expectation of the teller and the hearer.

Words are a habitation.

The meter reads all nines.

At this extremity all instruments of order fail. Paint peels from
my Mondriaan. The type in the books fades into indecipherable
glyphs, or falls into permutations of some dozen consonants, or
repeats the same word a thousand times. There is a volume titled
Stories, tales of people like myself, unlike myself: I read them
when the weight of the present oppresses, and when the weight
of reading oppresses I write in the blank pages at the end, in-
venting others like myself, unlike myself. In this book I have
never found the same story twice, they appear without title or
signature, I find pieces of my own writing set in their midst,
and don't know whether to read this as confirmation or loss. It
may be that I am no man at all, but a construct of ideas, perhaps
the fragmentary idea of an Author who was reluctant to be
created but had, after all, no choice. Then I would be last to
fall—unless, in addition to narrating I am also narrated, locked
in the chambers of my own narrator's subjectivity, as those I
describe are locked in mine. I can look at pages I have written
with no memory of writing them, nor understanding of them;
am I likewise a forgotten or lapsed synapse of connection in

some other mind? Perhaps I am not here as an observer, as object, but as subject. Perhaps I was accused rather than nominated.

He has stopped going forward, at least through the rooms. Now he spends fruitless days in one place, reading. The books, for all their veneer of helpfulness, of order, of knowledge, are full of factitious detail about some other reality that is baffling and frustrating. Tiresomely they describe people and places that he can never know. He has wasted so many days in as many rooms looking, in their pages, for a way out. When he comes to himself after hours of reading, he hardly recognizes where he is and feels vaguely cheated, traduced, by the books or by his reality or by his inability to bring them together or keep them apart. Language has had its way with him but has left him alone and unsuccored when done with him.

It is increasingly difficult to keep records. The lights fade and flare. It is night over the ocean in my last window, and when the lights die I sit in unmarked darkness and await their return, in terror, with pen held absolutely still, in faith and fear that I might continue; a wind comes, black and intense, through the walls, my skin, my thoughts, open mouth to speak, then calm again, the light returns.

It is increasingly difficult to keep records. Books, paper, voice. At this extremity all instruments of order fail. I walk to the edge. The wind cuts through me. Like one possessed I return and let the wind speak, all words, all voices but mine, but yours. I can't hear your words, too far and faint, can't tell what you want. Either you know everything, in which case my imprisonment here is monstrous, or you know nothing, in which case my report cannot be faulted. Or else you know a little. I have been sent to increase your knowledge, and you too are fallible, you will understand my difficulties. I have never attempted to deceive, just to escape, though I know full well escape is impossible, the room, the walls, the door that vanishes cunningly when you shut it, you could spend your life there, in the twilight, you can speak forever or say nothing, all voices present, unheeded. At the shore.

Rosenbloom, thinks Rosenbloom, is a constructed being. Each of his cells contains a unique strip of DNA from each individual of Earth's tired masses. Billions of codes within his billions of cells. When the ship reaches light speed Rosenbloom will enter an unaging suspension while it seeks a habitable planet. Rosenbloom will dream in a billion voices. Like the Prince of the Dharma in a legend he has read, he will wander among the stars of the Dipper, also called the Seven Sleepers, seeking his ancestral grove. When the ship sets down Rosenbloom will be dismantled, cell by cell, his proteins loosed to spice the new world's Protean stew: a scum of enzymes atop its virgin sea. And millions of years hence another Rosenbloom will face a new exhaustion on this alien world.

They should not have dispatched agents to such diverse points without providing against their return. If they come, from a million remote chilly outposts, from physics, anthropology, epistemology, absolute music, pure math, pure myth, from regions they've yet to hear of, if they come from literature, genetics, eschatology, teleology, cybernetics, taxonomy, historiography, number theory, they will have to devise a common speech of impossible complexity. Perhaps they'll send out more, to linguistics, information theory, semiotics, grammatology, thermodynamics, phonetics, syntactics, mimetics, and each end, each collapse of order, will found a new science of decay. They should have realized from the start, when they created gravity and let things fall, it could come only to this, the mountains fall to sand, the stars drop from the sky like stones, the bright elements decay to lead, clear from the beginning that in the end would be only silence, complete, irrevocable, all order of disruptions played still at last, because time is only the direction of our decay, we can't know it until the final moment when there is no more time, no more fear, no more hope, no more words, that moment is always immanent, inevitable, unless by some inversion the dead cold atoms and philosophies all jerk erect and start again, that's plausible, if time is a difference of potential, between high order and low, falling from the clouds, past the eyries, the cliffs, in runnels, rivulets, streams, rapids through the foothills, meanders through the flatlands, to the delta, the shore, the ocean salted with change and decay, to encircle islands, this one, every moment lived is a new shore despite its resemblance to every other moment except perhaps the last moment, unique, when heat is no longer heat, death no longer death, in the last moment when time shivers to a halt, when all things and times are at last equal, uniform diffuse ash, space itself flat as glass, in this ataxy opposites might resolve, the poles might reverse, perfect chaos might yield to perfect order, and the slow slide to silence start anew, more time, more fear, more hope, more words, another go-round, what's worse, death or eternity, the twilight offers both, too long to let one escape saying the words and too short to validate anything but silence.

Bodies. He finds them lying on the floor, seated at desks, hanging by their heels, decapitated, dismembered, nude, in period costume, preserved or decomposed, all with expressions of dismay, excepting of course those headless or too far gone for expression to matter. Oddly, there is no smell.

They might not be real. They might be a pleasant fiction he has constructed, persons whose presence in the rooms is more pointless than his own. They might be others like himself, who have come this far before dying. They might be those hapless ones described in the books, with their lives so unlike his, discarded it may be by their reality into his. Cause for hope: he could find himself discarded into theirs.

It began with that damned Englishman, he put me on his machine, the twinkling sensation of darkness and light was excessively painful to the eye. In one fantastic instant, centuries of ordered thought were annihilated. Presently as I went on still gaining velocity the palpitation of night and day merged into one continuous grayness. The peculiar risk lay in the possibility of my finding some substance in the space which I, or my fictions, occupied. So long as I traveled at a high velocity through time, this scarcely mattered; but to come to a stop, to invent a fiction, involved the jamming of myself, molecule by molecule, into whatever lay in my way: meant bringing my atoms into such intimate contact with those of the obstacle that a profound chemical reaction—possibly a death of hope—would result, and blow myself and my artifices out of all possible dimensions— into the Unknown.

Or it began with that expatriate Englishwoman, the one who insisted science could create life, that ideas could be given flesh, not from a first cause, or from the magics of fiction, but from bodies, fragments long dead and decayed, stitched with threads of technology and romance, on a bet, tell us a ghost story, aren't there ghosts enough, don't we haul a train of them behind us daily without letting on that we exhume them purposely, rob graves, steal parts for our own dark ends, and bind them, these heterogeneous limbs, with words and dark intent? Or I was born in the year 1632, my father had a small estate in Nottinghamshire, I was the third of five sons, of a good family, though not of that country, I saw the hideous phantasm of a man stretched out, and then, on the working of some powerful engine show signs of life, and stir with an uneasy, half-vital motion, was I exceedingly surprised with the print of a man's naked foot on the shore, mine or another's, we've been here before, and I alone am escaped to tell thee. . . . The moon? Gravity rules all the way out to the cold sphere, there is always the danger of falling.

I have been here before. Wherever there is uncertainty, wherever there is some edge to be explored, wherever knowledge has reached a limit and someone must wade into the sea of ignorance surrounding, I am sent. I am all those called upon to speak for those unwilling to speak for themselves, all narrators of all fictions, here at an edge of time, a shore, where all fictions tend, all structures which attempt in their way to deny or affirm time, whether the works of Beethoven or the victims of Genghis Khan or a small chip in a machine oscillating at four hundred fifty-five kilohertz or a molecule of inert gas at a certain temperature and pressure or the inventions of Thomas Alva Edison. I am all this. I am the ablative case of the grammar of a forgotten language, and all the acts of a secret police in a country of a hundred million, and the *Journal of Experimental Physics* for 1957, I am the theorems of Heisenberg and Gödel, and the Mississippi River of all who have never seen it, I am every evasion or encapsulation of the real, here where you sent me, as you sent others elsewhere to tell you what something else was like, afraid to go yourselves, I am them too, the consequence and the last end of every word, deed, and intention, I am all this, filtered through the particular space and time of your listening, the cat's-whisker of your attention, culture, and private failure, nor will this document last, nor will you be able to recall it, except at the edge of dreams, nor will I speak in this voice again, but I will never fall silent, the voice, the wind, through a million other filters, a million other spaces, times, cultures, languages, will be heard until their last end, if any.

The still point. All instruments read zero. Lotuslimbed Rosenbloom squats on the ship's floor. Lanky Einstein enters, with a beer, expounding unity of space, time, gravity. He insists further on the unity of personalities, hence all questions and quests. He tells Rosenbloom that he might as well be sitting at home puzzling over a false cognate, or in an eighth-century monastery debating over angels, or writing, say, a science fiction story. All edges equal, all inquiries the entangled atoms of a single body of inquiry. He unbolts the port to reveal the stars hung like fruit in the sky. Rosenbloom would like to stay in this peaceful garden at the end of speed, at this velocity where, as soulful Albert points out, mass becomes infinite, space and light bends to you, all messages collapse inward upon themselves, stay, with his nose pressed against the glass of this noumenal, numinous florescence, among the sprays of hyperbolas, n-spaces, tachyons, and forgetfulness cool against the black, a still, distant light refracted through the cosmos' saddleshaped vase; but a vertigo takes him, and he knows that he is returning. The mechanisms have functioned as intended, and they are taking him home. It depresses him to be again an occupant of history. Quickly words and names return: arithmetic, astronomy, geometry, music, grammar, logic, rhetoric; avarice, envy, gluttony, lechery, pride, sloth, wrath; Adrastus, Amphiarus, Capaneus, Hippomedon, Parthenopaeus, Polynices, Tydeus. Minor man, he carries no freight of dreams out to a new world, but comes back like Crusoe to write his dull detailed report, and face for the millionth time the agony of the particular. The Romans and the Klamath Indians had the same word for wind. The heart of his mind flies toward its maker, waves toward a shore, sparks into the sky, as if wisdom could be reached by traversing orts of knowledge like miles, as if there were any other way. Laboriously he will build from the words of others, found objects, the castle and prison of his own destiny.

Today. Last window gone. I awoke to find it in shards on the floor. So strong the sense of change. The overhead lights so bright they hurt my eyes.

Wind spirals through the chambers, and outside, a mist of rain blurs my view of the edge. I sense the world softening like gelatin, the edge crumbling like an ice floe in spring. My face is wet. The rain stings. Perhaps in striking it expends the binding energy of matter. Listen: in the courtyard I arrange clamshells in a spiral; as they fill, the pitch of striking droplets deepens. They speak random words, they speak of summer in the mountains, the quiet high Alps, so still the sound of cowbells drifted miles across the valleys in the cool air, over constellations of wildflowers on the green slopes, past the snow melting far above, the bells' lax tingling, like days in my childhood (when? where?) when rain seemed to enclose the day, to reduce all future time to domestic size, and even then I would fright at the thought of the rain getting inside and claiming me. But that fear is past, and in the memory is no longing. It is colder now. I am without desire.

List: lest lost lust last. I am without desire. The wind strips trees and borrows from bare boughs its speech. Snow slips through my walls, collects in corners, the air rife with its smell, a hard clean chemical scent of void. The sea heaves under a dancing screen of white. The roar of surf, noise, static, overwhelms. I have been here before. List. Snow falls and the falling is a stasis, a silence. Today. Last. All falls.

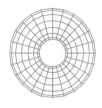

THE NINE BILLION NAMES OF GOD

Dear Mr Scholz,

Regarding your submission, "The Nine Billion Names of God": I shouldn't even bother to respond, but I don't want you to think that I'm gullible. Plagiarism occurs in science fiction as elsewhere, but I've never before seen anyone submit a word-for-word copy of another story, let alone a story as well-known as Arthur C. Clarke's "The Nine Billion Names of God." For you to imagine that any editor could fail to recognize this story implies a real ignorance of, and contempt for, our field. In the future I will not welcome your submissions.

Sincerely,
Robert Sales
Editor
NOVUS Science Fiction

Dear Mr Sales,

Well, this is what comes of submitting without a cover letter. Of course I knew you would recognize Clarke's story, and I hoped that you would infer the reasoning behind my story, which I freely admit is word-for-word the same as Clarke's. Nonetheless, there are important differences, which I shall explain.

First, this story could not have been written today. Too much of the internal evidence is against it. If a reader recognizes the story, the clue is obvious, and the disorientation is instant. Otherwise, an uneasiness will grow at mention of the "Mark V computer" with its "thousands of calculations a second," the "electromatic typewriters," "Sam Jaffe," and other obvious anachronisms.

On top of this, I have avoided using the conventional meanings of words. For example, when I use "machine," I intend "a vast and barren expanse of land" or "an outmoded philosophical system." Naturally this presents difficulties. The invention (or redefinition) of words is nothing new to science fiction, but I doubt if it has ever been done on this scale, where every single word in a story has a meaning unique to that story. (The new meanings are all tabulated in a glossary that I chose not to submit, economy being the first virtue of art; a short story with explanatory notes the length of a novel would be ridiculous.)

So there is enough depth here to interest a reader. There is the "mask" of the Clarke narrative, behind which lurks my own narrative, told in my "invented" language, and behind that is the story of my story: how a contemporary work of prose came to resemble superficially a science fiction story of the 1950s. These are deep questions of context; as the identical arrangement of letters (such as *elf* or *pain*) may mean differently in different languages, so my arrangement of words "means" very differently than Clarke's.

There is more, but I think this sufficient for now. The story is difficult, I admit, but not inaccessible. I think your readers are intelligent enough to deal with it.

Of course, I understand your reluctance. After all, if I may say so, your publication has gained a certain reputation for stodginess, and your more conservative readers would probably find "The Nine Billion Names of God" too avant-garde.

Yours,

Carter Scholz

Dear Mr Scholz,

Are you for real? Are you saying you've used the words of Clarke's story to stand in, one-for-one, for other words, like a cryptograph? It's absurd. I don't believe a word of it. Even the idea is derivative. I'm sure I've seen it in Borges. In its most basic form this notion of changing the context of an artifact might make a readable story, but certainly not this way.

There's no need to blame my "conservative" readers for the rejection. Just blame me.

Sincerely,
Robert Sales

Dear Mr Sales,

Since you ask, here is the revised ms. As you can see, no words have been changed, but experience should teach you to look further. I have revised my glossary and appendices, and changed some rules of grammar, along with quite a lot of the history of the world from which this artifact purports to come. Also—a nice touch, I think—the articles in the story have all been restored to their original meanings. "A" is "a," "the" is "the," etc.

There is so much information in the world already that I find it more revealing to create new contexts than new information. It would be more accurate to compare my work to Warhol or Duchamp than Clarke or Borges, whom in any case I have not read.

Sincerely,
Carter Scholz

Dear Mr Scholz,

Incredible. I had no idea you would resubmit "your" story—with "revisions", no less! I am re-returning it. I don't want to see it again, ever. I don't care if it's "really" derivative of Duchamp or Warhol or Gustave Flaubert. Just leave me alone.

RS

Dear Mr Sales,

This time I'm lowering my sights a little. I think you'll find this story really funny. It's a kind of "parody-by-repetition." This kind of parody is effective with works of a "baroque" nature, that is, works based on the logical, exhaustive permutations of a few principles. Science fiction stories are "baroque" because they are the intellectual children of empiricism, so they tend to offer explanations, and they tend to exhaust a limited repertoire of materials. The ambition of explanations is to be complete, so such systems tend to be closed, and this closure leads naturally to repetition and counterfeiting, endlessly evident in rack after rack of books about plucky young wizards or wisecracking starship tailgunners. The sportive elan of early science fiction has spiraled into an abortive ennui, and its writers face an endgame situation, where the remaining moves are few and predictable. Clarke's monks naming the names of God from AAAAAAAA to ZZZZZZZZ (with the help of a computer) no more surely faced the end of their world. My "counterfeit" of Clarke is more interesting, more purely "speculative" than this other sort of plagiarism. Here, the very act of quoting becomes parody, much like the act of moving a soup can from the supermarket to a gallery. It makes ridiculous the soup, the gallery, the audience, and the artist. It unites them.

Sincerely,
Carter Scholz

PS. There are several refinements in this draft. I hope you don't think I'm overworking it. Since each time I submit it its context is changed, of course you are not really seeing the "same" "story" "again." There are no "agains" in this game.

Dear Mr Scholz,

No! I see no changes in the story, but you are definitely overworking me!

You seem to have a good mind. Why not do something constructive with your time? Save yourself postage and save me grief.

Yours, again, still, and for the last time,
Bob Sales

"Dear" "Mr" "Sales,"

A "text" "admits of" numerous "interpretations." The "interpretations" "become" more "numerous" as "time" "passes." Most "important," "it" seems to "me," is the "act" of "reprinting" "The Nine Billion Names of God" "today". "Presenting" it in that "context" "sets up" a "series" of "speculations" more "interesting" than those "raised" by most of the "stories" "you" "publish." This "matter" of "context" is a kind of "Last Question" for "art", "literature," and "ultimately" "science fiction." The "real" "story" always "lies" "outside" the "words"—in "context", "implication," and "association"—in what is "not" "written." "Surely" "you" can "see" "that"? Let "us" be "brave," and "pursue" the "implications" of "our" "activities."

"Sincerely,"
"Carter Scholz"

Dear Mr Scholz,

How would it be if I bought the story and didn't publish it? Would that get you off my back? The quotes in your last letter gave me eyestrain, and I'm beginning to dread opening my mail.

Yours,
Sales

Dear Mr Sales,

Since I am obviously among friends, since you understand that words mean only what we are conditioned to think they

mean (legitimated in dictionaries according to the biases of lex-
icographers), I will dispense with the quotes. And I will tell you
something which I previously withheld. My story, "The Nine
Billion Names of God," was generated by a computer. But let
me approach this new development by stages.

Like any number of people (your mailbox must be jammed
with their efforts), I once thought I would like to write science
fiction. For several years I worked at it, until the notion had
passed from a hobby to an avocation to a passion to an obsession.
Never has so much energy been turned to such small account.
I failed, utterly, exhaustively, repeatedly; daily, yearly, by degrees
and in large lots, I failed. I collected a tower of rejections in-
forming me it had all been done better, and probably with less
effort, by Clifford Simak or Curt Siodmak in 1947. And in
truth, looking over my millions of failed words, I could no
longer tell whether they were very much better, very much
worse, or about the same as the published works I had set out
to emulate.

By now I was not in my right mind. Have you ever lain
awake at night, repeating a simple word like "clown" over and
over, until it loses its meaning? Entire stories reached that insane
pitch for me. In my sleep I would get rejection letters about
my own dreams. Only a long course of therapy brought me
back to a point where I could, more or less, construct sentences.

So I gave it up and went back to school.

My graduate studies were about randomness. In one course
I made a random number program to simulate the motion of
gas molecules in a closed space. By varying the "temperature"
of the space I could control the degree of randomness. I used
the numbers to select words from a dictionary, and generate
random texts; late at night I found their incoherence soothing.
But one night, in the midst of this placid gibberish, the machine
suddenly gave out the complete text of "The Nine Billion
Names of God."

As in cliché fiction, the hackles did stand on my neck. I printed the pages. I checked the network in vain for any sign of a prankster.

I shut down the machine and went home. There I compared my printout to the published Clarke text. Word for word it was the same. There was nothing strange about it, except for where and how it had appeared. After a few stiff drinks, I began to feel lighthearted. For there it was, at last, the product of my labors, a vindication, a light at the end of a closed universe, the abnihilisation of the etym, the big bang. I had produced a real science fiction story, and a certified classic, at that! However obliquely, I had become a science fiction writer; I had, in fact, with exactly the same words, achieved more subtlety, depth, and irony than Clarke himself. How could I doubt it? For, unlike Clarke's story, mine could be verified at the atomic level.

Well, I thought to give myself the Fields Prize for math and a Nebula Award for best story. In a fever I devised my histories, glossaries, and so on, as I have previously explained. I created a unique context for an extant text, a story as commonplace in the world of science fiction as Campbell's soup is to *tout le monde*.

Running the program backwards, by the way, produced Asimov's "The Last Question."

But this brings me to the central problem. If gas molecules (or their stand-ins), capering at random, can produce a pattern equivalent to the pattern of words in "The Nine Billion Names of God," or "The Last Question," or indeed in time any text, even those not yet written—then why write? An author publishes from doubt, I think; he wants the world to regard him as real, substantial, genuine. But in this case, does such confirmation matter? Can one persuade molecules?

The pattern of any story can be found in the random phenomena of nature. The air hums. Daily the ten thousand things recite all nine billion names. A rainstorm, a gust of wind, the bending of a tree, heat waves, all are instinct with a wisdom beyond signs, more engaging than any story because they encompass and can engender all stories. You may find a story in a tree, but never a tree in a story, only the constellation of letters *tree*, and the crushed remains of one in the paper. Why tell stories if all the stories that ever could be are told constantly in the wind and the rain? That is the real last question: do we need fiction? do we need science?

I labored years with my ambition, and have learned that it is pointless. The end of ambition is to end ambition, just as the point of a fiction is to subsume lesser fictions, and the end point of all fiction is to reach that supreme fiction, the world. Though not without a journey.

But we have taken that journey before. In our stories we have gone past Mercury and Pluto; inclined in worshipful orbit to our great gods Speed and Death, those creators and annihilators of meaning, we have turned a thousand times in a thousand tales. We have seen the engines of our imagination actually built and lifted into space, and they have not meliorated our plight. I think we may never reach a plain sense of things as long as we have either science or fiction to hide behind.

The story of the story of my story ends here. Believing this, I must withdraw my manuscript from submission. I hope you understand. I'd rather not see any more stories published anywhere.

Thank you for your interest.

Sincerely,
Carter Scholz

Dear Contributor:

We are returning your manuscript because publication of *NOVUS Science Fiction* has been discontinued. Thank you for your interest.

The Editor

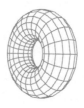

INVISIBLE INK

HELLO, WORD. No, that won't do. First rule's to fix the place and time. Start anew. The fancy stuff can be deferred.

A beach near San Diego, feast of same (11/13). Here am I, Charles Ochre by name, mediocre joker, safe starbore, fallow hack with shallow reach, any part of a swarm, in my shack by the bay, scrying apocalypse in bloody dusks, omens in the husks of eelskins shed. Diego, lay brother, friar minor, stand me now as ever in good stead.

First dream in many a day to vex my sleep. Rose and I are swimming. The water's deep, the sky is gray and dimming. Rain flecks the sea. Cold waves stream in, pick up pace. I see her sweet head rise and fall. Her maillot shimmers blue, then she's lost to view. I'm tossed against a sheer rock wall. No handhold on its slick dark face.

Awoke with heart arace. Calmed it with a drink. Quake anxiety, I'd like to think. Nearly half my colleagues (seers and savants all) live, as I, on faulted earth. Hollow mirth. Colleagues, did I say, about this blight? That carries hints of law and right; cohort's better, from enclosure, as of sheep. (Sometimes my learning's deep.)

To beat insomnia I plotted out a book or two. O the things

a hardened pro can do. A dozen times a year I turn this trick; rare's the morning after I'm not sick.

Nepenthe for the moment. But now I read the aftermath. Scrawled notes infirm as rotten lath. A bridge best burned. I rise and cross my single room to search the fridge. Ozonekilling fluid mutters in its coils. The milk has turned. I take a beer and light a smoke. The toils of creation, what a joke.

But here's another rule already broken. No character we care about, no roguish fool, no wellmade lout with winsome grin. I know I sin against a creed observed wherever narrative is spoken, but I favor the face effaced, the immaculate deception. Would you rather have a closeup of my pores, some prolix hinting, some smug and tiresome blather? Do you need factitious detail like a drug? ZOOM IN on OCHRE's squinting mug as MUSIC swells in minor thirds. O sure. Forget it, learn to read. Cinema's the enemy of prose. I'm made of words, my camera's obscure. Let's have another character. Hello, Rose?

Met her at a cohort's party. He'd sold a book to that same silver screen, and had his fellow Gadarene over for a gloat. Nothing arty, same old scene. Ochre with his close and gripéd mien. Some minor movie sorts adding brassy charm. Rose, from the studio, was smiling past some boozy swine in a madras coat. (These men write books? They dress like unsuccessful crooks.) As I passed, she caught my eye; her arm found mine. A shock for the old goat. I'd blinked away her beauty: too young. Age, age is the canker that eats the heart and leaves a dry shell of dung. How soon it's late—the sagging flab, the graying pate, this tendency to blab and prate. She steered us out while I, oncebold cocksman, came dumbly along, my reason in rout.

What she saw in me, God knows—a change from all the up-and-comings, comeback kids, and hustlers that plagued her days. My selling point: I hadn't anything to sell. I seemed sincere, swell pose. She listened to my woes. How could such a love survive? But every weekend she makes the long drive from Burbank down the Five. To me. It continues to amaze, this roseate halo round the event horizon of my darkling life. No hole's so black it can't emit some radiance.

Fair morning. Best ideas are dawnbrought. Woes abate in sun-blessed air. Early I walk and shift among the ashes of my thought (that surly mess and billingsgate), then try (most often fail) to break my drought, to conjure some swift flashes and make a decent page of prose. Then drift up to Michael's Bar for my mail. And Bass Ale. I've no address, no phone, no heat; just my one-room shack. Michael cashes my checks and collects the rent for some drone I hope I'll never meet.

Grim message for me there. Our Great Man, the dean of future fiction, is dead. So: not San Andreas shook my bed, but my radar, keen as ever for travail. Wherever I've fled I never fail to get bad news, grim tidings from our harlot Muse. Why this grief? this mean contrition? I couldn't even read his stuff. To him one word was good as any other. I'd carp about his awful style; he'd give me an outlaw's smile, as if to say, same boat. True enough, it's my perdition. My esthetic guff's more frail than his rough faith; he just punched the clock and wrote. Still, a brother.

The book of my dead, my lost. Affection's cost. When I lived in Long Beach in a different shack (another chapter in my history of flight, another vain attempt to cope by staying hid), young Stephen came by unbid. He wanted to write. Better I'd shot him dead than offered any hope. He knew my books, admired—what? my hack malaise? my zircon turns of phrase? I listened to his praise, let myself be flattered. Son I'd never have, all that. I encouraged him, told him that it mattered. Fool! Hadn't I enough to rue? But what else could I do? I'm helpless before the true quill, blossom where it will. He'd talent, more

than I, a better mind, a voice more unconfined—he'd not make
my mistake. O no, he'd find his own. Each artist harrows hell
alone. Words have more power to break than to mend. The
Pierian spring's a site of human sacrifice. Let that suffice.

Theater's where I found my so-called voice. I studied with a
Young American Playwright, you know the breed (promising),
call this one Yap. Bad choice. I'd no feeling for the stage, but
that didn't stop me getting down to ukases: actors don't know
how to read; it's perverse to animate a page; Joyce, there's a
writer; *Exiles*, there's a play. Jaysus, that people put up with my
crap, today it makes me writhe. Back then I was impenetrably
blithe. With Yap's imprimatur I thought everyone from Papp
to Mabou Mines would greet me with glad cries, sing my
praises, vie to stage my lines. Graciously I'd clue them in to
what dramatic art was all about.

Intolerable lout. I found my level soon enough: Joseph
Stough, my agent to this day. I took what came along: quick-
buck paperbacks, one of a stable of hacks, under a name of the
pen (there's that enclosure again)—o shame, o bitter truth—for
Boring Books, Robert Owen Boring, proprietor. At least this
work would pay.

Lost youth. I thought my mind could labor while my soul
stayed chaste. Why not do a book or two? Don a mask; mum's
the word. Ten bucks a page, bare competence for living wage.
Simple task, future fiction, I could do it in my sleep. Many's
the shining ship I dreamed of as a child, its steep climb up
inkblack night on jets of fire, escaping what else but time's sentence writ in my young body's growth, a ripening whose promised end was not transcendence but rot.

ROB IOU, my giver of rules and deadlines and checks, pal-
adin of the reader-writer contract, chastener of the venturesome,
champion of the plain tale well told, defender of the sense of

wonder, mogul of the book twice sold. Each finished work
brought commission for the next. What a blunder. O how I could
invent for gold; a week each month would pay my rent. But invention's a surge no nobler than the peristaltic urge. Brethren, the
sleep of reason's not so deep. It got old. It began to gall.

So my fall. Thirty hit. My spendthrift life had shortened quite
a bit. Perhaps this stuff that ate my time wasn't pure dreck,
perhaps I ought to give it due respect, become a player in the
band. It could be something grand, or even—o tempora!—art!
Those fantasies of star tsars and planetary plenipotentiaries are
puerile perspectives, my boy, adventitious adventures all; but
consider the lilies of the field, how they blacken under Agent
Orange, consider how the comfort of the few is fed from all
our common lot, consider then the dispossessed, the ruined, the
bereft, the smiling prosperous face of theft, regard the torturers
employed by plutocrats to crush dissent, behold the shining engines grinding under iron treads the precincts of the sacred, consider the efficiencies of scale, how scientific knowledge and
financial gain dovetail, how vanity seduces thought, how
bought language chicanes, how love does fade while dross remains, how power's the supreme addiction. I was haunted. How
else write this poem of our loss, but using equal measures science
and fiction?

Need I say this poem was unwanted? Scriblerus writes *Man's
Fate*. Boring sent it back with naked hate. ROB IOU.

My last book, nothing daunted, was a travesty on all good
Bob held dear: *Oxen of the Stars*, a romp through hyperspace in
warp drive bumpercars and cyberprose, I fear, more fervid than
pen (that cell again!) can tell. The bogus pomp of a pseudoseer.
Like Simeon, seeking a new start, I climbed my pole. A style
for every planet! Mercurial, venereal, earthy, martial, steroidal,
jovial, saturnine, uranic, neptunian, and plutonic your man was
in turn, bat into hell to disport with shades, then out past Planet
X with a will, for this was farewell: last contract to fulfill, last

bridge to burn. *Vade retro me, futura.* I renounce thee and thy ways. Much to my amaze, Bob thought it was just swell. And your man walked off with accolades: a chromium rocket like a finny tube, a chunk of quartz in a lucite cube, and a career still spoken of (though seldom) as meteoric. Meteors, you know, fall.

How long ago that was. Stephen, veteran of our long bad Asian war, understood at once that these imagined spaceships, warp drives, time machines, and vast cool cybernetic minds were engines of the night. All our babble of transcendence was unpaid propaganda for the Moloch at the century's heart, that Might to which we sacrifice our virtues for a sup of godly vice. The shit of such gods is ambrosial; one taste excites unbounded appetite. Science is war's child and begetter. This his insight was my Damascus; scales fell from my eyes. In all my books I saw complaisant lies. To write them well was but to serve this power better.

So I quit, or tried to. Invisible I'd thought I was, not-I my truest name. Instead I'd found infame. Postmortems dogged me. Backlogged work came out, seemed new. Reviews lagged too. ("Ochre serves up his usual stew of halfbaked ideas and poached plots.") New editions, reprints, foreign pirates, rose up undead. In the year 2225 some hypertrophied vermin, new masters of the wasted Earth our cenotaph, survivors of some megabomb, will find Ochre's oeuvre on CD-ROM and have a good long snide chitinous laugh.

This wasn't what I had in mind. Work of this kind should fade from the page like disappearing ink as soon as it's made. Instead, like Wells's mad scientist, I stood revealed on bloody tiptoe in a field of broken glass, bareass, overweight. Some estate for a tired man in middle age.

Pull down vanity, I say, pull down. I went to ground. True

invisibility I found in work for hire: ad copy, corporate reports, tech manuals, assemblages of doubtful facts—the mire of commerce, the subworlds of the word next which my Boring Books were high Virgilian art. My namelessness was legion. Abnegation's what I sought. No signature meant no guilt—is that really how I thought? And, odd but true, the farther from Parnassus sunk, the more remunerative the junk.

All through this misbegotten penance I hoped the books would be forgotten. Did I think some black hole would swallow them without a trace, restore the mind that made them to a state of grace? Would my unsigned corporate pother swirl down some information sink and vanish with a slurp? Fat chance. A hole engorging matter gives a little burp. The matter must emerge: no addicted dancer can escape the dance. We're what we do, no better, and no other. The hole spit me out in Hollywood, hello.

Nel mezzo woody hell (though Dante's came at thirty). I quit my monkish cell. Think, I thought, of the millions who might view my poem of sedition (so far a strictly limited edition). Phew! Endless meetings, psychic beatings. Middling C, that's me, imperfect pitcher. My scripts were bought but never made. I was paid; I ended richer; so what the heck. Just a few more years of one note hunt and peck. How many ways can you spell QWERTY?

I cannot do it any more. I've heard the agents singing each to each; they cast their pearls past this swine's beach. Now I've only myself to offer and that fills no one's coffer.

Hola, San Juan de la Cruz (11/24)! Soul's night's no easier in California sun. What use is all this time alone? The minutes drag, the hours creep and skulk—yet years have flown.

Rose arrives for our holiday repast. From the kitchen nook come homey rattles and potpan clanks. Pressed into service, C, who tends to lunch on uncooked franks (I mention this, she gives a look), chops a bunch of thyme, nicks and sucks a fingertip. Rose trusses two wee hens for the toaster oven. Soon their smell fills the air. Sun gilds her hair, and for a moment I believe: this life is mine. I do give thanks.

Our feast is fine. After which Rose and proximate C sit on sagging planks (the porch) and sip our wine. Last light limns seawrack and seaspawn hanging on my walls, a gallery of castup junk: glazed bottle, abalone shell, rusted hasp, driftwood rune: stranger than any wonders on the moon. Not for me the stuff of abstract space or time—but a morning mist, a winter rain, the feel of Rose's wrist, tide running on a shoal—in short, the real—this is where I stake my soul.

Then Rose asks me: what happens if a spaceship enters a black hole? I know where this is heading. Subtle try to rectify my bootless ways, give me a goal: consultant, story editor, peevish jade, can't I find a trade that pays, and cease to mope? Faint hope. My mopery's ingrained. But here, my dear, black holes explained: my chrome prize rocket held erect, I, prize fool, dive for her sweet singularity. After a tussle we elect for my natural though punier tool. Glad joining of Cs, in a tangle of bedding.

But afterwards, finishing the chardonnay, she has to say: why can't I write? O crap. The question I've been dreading. I slap the half page in my Olympia, what's this then, elm blight? But she knows my kinks. Every time a story gets a head of steam I stop and say it stinks. How this fool's cap fits. I'm a sham of a Shem in my selfstyled sin, writing my woes with my shit on the sheet of my skin. But a book's a holy vessel, so I've heard; it can transubstantiate a turd.

Why not indeed? It's easy: open a vein and bleed. Flay flesh to bone and with flint of purpose strike brief flame. Rush the embers into print and enjoy your fame. O but my dear, write I can: not wisely but too well. It's this I fear, this scurrilous facility that's beached me here. I can't help myself going on.

Shall I foreswear futures for the diction of the moment, curry favor with the flavor of the year, urban schtick or country chic or some post-pomo trick? Talk about your science fiction, I wish I had such wiles. Or shall I try again to change the world, hi Rosinante! As well try leash a juggernaut. Shall I politize my thought, give my crabby notions winning smiles, like Dante in a Pulcinello mask? Run and yell like Henny Penny? I've tried both; nobody was having any.

Reader, co-respondent, are you really so benighted? Are my words as vain as seed spilled in a sterile sea? Not one can strike you sighted? Look at me, you ghostly swine, I'm done with tact, here's no anodyne, live up to your half of the contract! Compare that seamy bestsold swill to the life you lead. Or is it only at escape velocity you read?

And still I waste words in this hallowed wood. Wandering my beach, ear cocked for angelic speech. (O rocks, no one talks like that.) Ah, but they might. Grant that of the billions daily writing and revising the long novels of their lives one, just one, may get it right.

Hope, the Buddhists say, is last to go before enlightenment.

Alba. Dawn song of the blank page. Commander Ochre (ret.) of the Lost Planet Airmen puts in his daily stint at the hermitage.

The cross saltire is Andrew's sign (11/30). He was crucified but once on his; mine inflicts a million cuts a year: *le mot inepte, le voix prolixe*, must be struck down coldeyed. I marvel that I've kept on mending defects for so long, when nearly every word I write seems wrong. Some typists wear out *es* and *as*; the symbol of my days's the *x*.

Maybe a computer's what I need. That's it—MicroHack, DOSpassos, Bartle-B, GogolPlex, RiteStuff, MultiScreed— surely in this pack there's software that confects the sort of fluff

America wants to read. From ones and zeros can any tale unfold, any world be controlled. If progress is the goal, why, anything that counts must have a soul.

Heretic. You'll never make the canon with that class of cod. Better think of money than of God. You're broke, you creep, so eye the trends. (How about a future world where *everyone's asleep?*) Christ, I'm ill, so this is how it ends, leaning on the space bar, cleaning keys with a straight pin, surly as a char. Mend the world? Never mind it. Mend your holy underwear, if you can find it.

It's no way to earn a living. Ready cash is running low: five hundred dollars in the Mason jar. I've weathered worse but never with a mind so slow or temper so ungiving. Sell the car. Cross the border if you really want to vanish. I'd be a millionaire in pesos, though I'd need a course in Spanish. Say, how's the market for projective verse? Or join the order of St Francis, like pious Diego and Charles of Sezze. Impious am I? Sez who, bub? I'm even kind to beasts. I once took in a baby gull, fed him half a ton of chub. Cry ke-kay, he flew off without a backward look. Or was I the gull?

But here's a knocking at my gates. A suit with a hammer. Eyes like a gull. I'd like to feed him half a ton of chub. Condemned, he says, stepping back as if I'm Beelzebub. *¿Q-qué?* I stammer. Rezoned, he elaborates. Save it for Scrabble, fink. I peek at the eviction notice, backdated a week. *¡Madre de Dios!* I implore. What would the Prince of Peace think? I do my taxes on December 24. But gulleye's gone.

Enough, Ochre, now relax. What's your shack? Echo chamber for morose keenings. Fortress of delay for the chronically unwilling. Don't damn God, that grand old hack, he's just another story where we cadge our meanings. Heal thyself, you quack. Build a pine box in remembrance of the four lost things: wife, art, home, and youth. Lay out in it your paltry gleanings.

Make it thrilling. Render your experience like fat to one smug
oily truth, anoint the corpse, sell book club rights, and make a
killing.

Poem of the planet, what a crock. Put paid to your charade,
it's vain, it's ended. *Acta Sanctorum*'s dull enough, God knows,
without your pipsqueak schlock appended. Admit that martyrs
need their pain.

Out early for my run, with jouncing gut. That pinpoint pain
again. The sky's a jewel cut by sun from bright air.

My love asked me to live with her and I said no. How share
this shabby character of mine, this masked and lackheat life? Diet
of hard cheese, dried meat, cheap wine, canned crab, chronic
mumming of Diogenes? Yet I'm sick, so sick, of squandering
my years. I've had and lost one wife, an almost-son, two half-
careers—what a litany of defeat. Happiness so long ago. Rose
mustn't pay the way for such a cheat.

To Michael's for my mail. Letter from the Joseph Stough
Agency. O frabjous day! Money, bucks, smirks carmine Wendell
Holmes, struck through by 90024 LA. Don't rip the check, eh
Chuck? What check? St Joe's epistle to the slob is all: get a job.

Dear Charles, I know you must be running short of funds,
ever the accountant Joe, and I wish I had something to send
you, of course you do since ten percent of nothing's nothing.
I wish as well you would reconsider your retirement, ah the
bullshit Christ it comes. I believe I can get you a substantial
advance from Ad Astra Press, a recent acquisition of Exxon, God
I'll weep, despoilers never sleep. They have expressed interest,
sure they'd cozen a quahog if it could hold a pen. I make no
promises, why not? Don't skimp, but your name is better
known than some who have gotten fifty thousand for hardcover
rights, now that's enough you lying pimp, fifty thou for a silk

purse from this sow? The only hard covers I'll ever have are the ones they put on to discourage worms. Stough, why do you persist, you've made enough from me, now write me off your list. Charles, the only constraint is a very short deadline, my very specialty, of course you'd think of me good Joe, and the traditional narrative values of the editor Robert Boring, what? What's this? ROB old friend, old thief, you've struck the mother lode, you gutless toad. First time tragedy, second time farce; *vita longa amplum arse.*

Thomas, doubter (12/21), had to lay hands on the resurrected Christ before he'd buy the tale. Michael, Bass Ale.

Stephen's feast day, protomartyr (12/26). Saul of Tarsus witnessed that death. Good will to the sheriff who's granted me a stay. A week more to catch my failing breath.

Sky bleak and gray; rain dripping from the beams. Feet in the electric fire. Run the bill up, what the hey, I won't be here to pay. I stare at half a page of halfremembered dreams.

So long ago. His novel sold. He called me when he got the galleys. He asked, is this success? More or less, I think I said. Get started on your second; look out for blind alleys. A month later he was dead, a suicide. Why? I still don't know. Damage from the war? He used a gun. Certainly not sins of pride. Art can't kill. Error's in things not done, or done ill.

Christ, I'm cold. So long ago, yet he persists, the pest, saying: go on, old man, just do your best. Damn you, Stephen, let me off the hook, don't make me write another lousy book. Damn you too, Chuck, heedless keeper of your talent that you've been. Have you written one true word? Do you think so late to start? How much time is left? Check your Bollandist chart.

I know how much I've done ill. But to have done instead of not doing, Stephen: this is not vanity.

———————

To his agential potency Joseph Stough:

Here have I writ an outline, and a goodly. Not for gold (though gold stayeth after love fadeth) but for the satisfaction of your honor. And it findeth in your sight a fraction of the favor I have had from your constant friendship, all my woe and worry is forgotten.

Till the Destroyer of Delights and Desolator of Dwelling-places translate us both to the ruth of almighty Allah, and our houses fall waste and our palaces lay in ruins and kings inherit the work of our hands, believe me to be,

Signed this *dies natalis* of the Holy Innocents (12/28).

PS. Fifty grand and not a penny less!

Simeon Stylites, flagpole sitter (1/5). Perched on a stack of crap outside the shack with feline Fog complaining in my lap. All my worldly goods—sagging boxes, beat-up table, collected works, more muck from the Augean stable—piled up like talus at the angle of repose. Awaiting what? A pickup truck. I'm moving in with Rose.

Brute cold morn. Sea wind bitter in my eyes, I blink back tears. A gull stalls and veers. Is it the same? Those callous cries. Cat calls back cattily. Below me something falls: volume 3 of the Collected Works. Hurry up, you jerks, I'll start to rave like Pascal; infinite space is nothing to the ruined palace of the hermit brain. Save me, brothers; greatly have I sinned, and will again. Christ it cuts, the wind!

Show some guts. Bear your chalice safely through a throng of foes. Old Yap once soothed me: when you need to write again, you will. I'm older now than he was then. So much waste. Rose, make haste! A minute more and I'll be winter kill.

At last. She sees me perched, she's, Christ, she's laughing, can't stand straight. Merriment at the raised-up reprobate. Insolent tart! I yell with heat. Show some respect! Apologize! Wind crams words back down my pipe. My black mood's wrecked, I'm grinning like a cheat, I wipe my eyes, my heart's elate. What's this, epiphany? No, only the beginning; I've never had a one complete. And revelation without a feast's a mere twelfthnight. Start the bone fire: a cold one this will be.

My time apart is done. And with it hope of art? Contract nestled at my breast. Hard won. Let me do my modest best.

My life that seemed so infinite, half gone at least. The end of quests is neither *urbs aeterna* nor the Beast, but just another start. Anything to hold the dark at bay. The ruth of the tumor. The length of the sentence.

The new book will be out in May.

MENGELE'S JEW

AT A Party function, Dr. Josef Mengele corners Werner Heisenberg, the physicist. Isolated as he is at Auschwitz, that *anus mundi*, Mengele seizes every opportunity to keep up with the most recent scientific developments. He prides himself on knowledge that extends even to atomic physics, while other medical men are content to remain glorified pharmacists.

—Suppose you have a cat in a box, says Heisenberg. —This little paradox, by the way, comes from my friend Erwin Schrödinger.

—Ah, Schrödinger. What a loss to German science, says Mengele.

—In the box is a mechanism. It holds a radioactive nucleus that may or may not decay according to the laws of quantum probability after, say, one minute. A Geiger counter detects any such decay, and triggers a hammer, which breaks a capsule of poison gas. After a minute, there is a fifty percent chance that the nucleus decays. Now, is the cat alive or dead?

Mengele thinks. The question must be subtler than it seems. Anxiously he studies the physicist's fine Aryan features, the reddish blond hair combed straight back, the eyes twinkling under heavy brows.

—But surely, there is a fifty percent chance . . . ?

—So one would think. But in the sealed box, the cat is neither alive nor dead. The cat is in a mixed state, composed of overlapping probability waves.

—That is because we cannot see into the box . . .

—No, no, it is not a matter of incomplete knowledge. It is the way things are.

—This is stupendous! Mengele is thunderstruck. He literally falls back a pace. At once an objection forms in his sharp mind. —But when one opens the box . . .

—At that moment, the two waves converge, and the cat lives or dies.

—Merely by the act of observation!

—That's one interpretation.

—And if one never opens the box?

—Then I suppose, the cat remains in limbo, though Einstein rejects this interpretation. He finds it too idealist.

—Einstein, says Mengele pointedly, —is a jew.

Heisenberg regards him for a moment, then turns away. Across the room Himmler is speaking. —It's easy enough to say, the jewish race is being exterminated, this is our program and we're doing it. But most of you know firsthand what it means when a hundred corpses are lying side by side, or five hundred, or a thousand. Not so easy. To have stuck it out and at the same time to have remained decent fellows, this is a page of glory in our history that will never be written.

Mengele is bored by the speech, though his handsome features remain alert. The graceful hand at his side flickers right, left, like an electron between energy levels, or as though he is conducting a Wagner aria.

In São Paulo, in the Estrada da Alvaranga, Mengele lies wearily on a bed in a tiny room. His hair is white, his breathing labored. His aching legs can barely support his weight, so he spends most of each day recumbent. In the evenings he takes a light meal that Elsa prepares for him. Sometimes he listens to the radio. Last night he found a station from the south, the announcer's voice deep in static, *a nona sinfônia de Beethoven regeda por Wilhelm Furtwängler*. It took him back to 1943 Berlin: the chorus of blond straightbacked youths like feverish angels following Furtwängler's frantic beat through Schiller's verse, *alle Menschen werden Brüder*, rushing as if to some divine consummation, *seid umschlungen Millionen*, gilt eagles glinting in the hall's dim light, and the tears came, for the beauty of the music, but also for the loss of that bright, pure Aryan world.

Daylight falls through the dusty window. Grime and paint have sealed it shut. The air is close and warm. The narrow room holds only a cot and a night table. Mengele keeps the door shut and locked from inside. Weatherstripping at the doorsill presents a barrier to insects, but some inevitably get in. Even now a fly crawls across the day's *Estado da São Paulo*, onto Speer's memoirs, books by Hannah Arendt and Martin Buber, and Mengele's own notebook.

Near the books is a curious device. He has been forced to modify Schrödinger's description, but Mengele is not without ingenuity. For the hammer and the vial of poison gas he has used a rat trap with a springloaded arm. A canister of hydrocyanic acid sits under its cocked arm so that the arm, when tripped, will snap down and break the valve, releasing the gas. So powerful is the spring, it takes all Mengele's strength to draw it back.

The only problem with cyanide gas, with Zyklon B, is that it goes bad. Fortunately his apparatus needs little, but every few months he sends an agent to buy more from a fumigator. The family chemical and farm equipment business in Buenos Aires still sends him money, but he gets his cyanide elsewhere. He suddenly wonders if the current canister is fresh. As he lifts his head, the fly springs into the air, buzzing. In the jaws of the trap, the canister's expiration date faces him. The date is yet to come. He shuts his eyes, his head falls back onto the pillow.

The sealed box in which this device will rest is still imaginary, but an outline has begun to form. First Mengele noticed the ladder at the foot of the bed, less a presence than a suggestion. From day to day it grew more definite, like the onset of some disease, some vague malaise that precedes true symptoms, until at last he accepted its reality. The ladder is of hewn wood lashed with hemp rope. It leans against the wall, so clear now that it attracts one's touch which, however, meets only air. Mengele has complained to Elsa of cobwebs in that corner, and she has swept and dusted around and through the ladder, but she has seen nothing. So, the doctor concludes, it is a matter of his superior perceptions.

The ladder leads to a trapdoor in the ceiling. Though tightly closed, the trapdoor somehow affords a view into the cell above it. And the cell, Mengele has realized, is no more or less than the observation tower of his old Serra Negra house—the same six-foot cube from which he so often surveyed that dismal neighborhood. The tower has somehow been transported from Serra Negra to São Paulo.

Last of all to become visible was the jew, sitting slumped in a chair above Mengele's head. It worries Mengele that he is able to see the jew inside the cell, but so far it seems all right, for the jew is quite immobile: impossible to tell if he's alive or dead.

The problem of introducing his real device into this imaginary cell remains to be solved. The question of the trigger is also unanswered—he has no radioactive material, nor a Geiger counter—but that is of little concern, for it is not the outcome that matters. Quite the opposite. Mengele is interested only in the mixed state that obtains before the cell is opened, the mixed state during which quantum possibility is infinite and undecided.

The jew's outline is vague and shifting. It variously takes the form of a young woman, a toothless old man, twin children.

This variety baffled him at first, but reflection made all clear. In Schrödinger's simplified box, there are two cats: one alive, one dead. But a more complex and subtle trigger would engage further conditionals. Two, four, eight, countless intermediate states come into being. Armies, races of ghosts multiply and march forth to await some final determination. With a device of sufficient intricacy, judgment could be put off indefinitely.

In Berlin, Himmler is done speaking. Heisenberg, expressionless, applauds with the rest. Mengele leans toward him.

—But surely the cat knows. Is not the cat's consciousness sufficient to resolve the uncertainty?

—Hm? Well, who knows, maybe not. It's only a cat.

—But if you put a man in the box.

This recaptures Heisenberg's interest. —Wigner raised the same point.

—And what does Wigner say? Mengele racks his memory. Ah yes: Eugene Wigner, another physicist. Hungarian. Probably a jew. It is astounding that Heisenberg, with his questionable friends, holds the high position he does. But, of course, Heisenberg's mother is friends with Himmler's mother. The applause fades, the band stumbles into a Strauss waltz.

—To Wigner it's a matter of consciousness. Only when the meaning of an observation enters the consciousness of an observer do the probability waves collapse to reality. This places a rather grave responsibility on living things with consciousness. Perhaps cats are spared this responsibility.

—So men are conscious, though cats are not. What about jews?

Heisenberg's smile is pained. —Excuse me, I must go.

Mengele thinks, if two observers are involved in the same system, each has the power to collapse it to reality. The occupant of the box observes the mechanism before the experimenter does. That's a problem. But suppose the occupant is ignorant of the meaning of the experiment. Then even as gas floods the box, his perceptions are not scientific observations.

The afternoon is dim, chill, cloudy. On the wind comes a heavy, sweetish smoke. From the camp's observation tower, Mengele sorts the new arrivals. Below him, guards split the line in two. Those fit to work, or those specimens holding some interest for his researches, he directs to the right with a minute flick of his gloved hand. The remainder, to the left. The guards usher them along, this way, don't worry, we're going to disinfect you with a nice hot shower. *Reinheit macht frei.* A Strauss waltz plays on the loudspeakers. Mengele's pointing finger, right, left, keeps a kind of time.

Camp rules insist that a doctor certify the results of the disinfection. Not so easy, as Himmler observed, to remain a decent fellow after that. He has seen it so many times, through the peephole: hundreds of jews packed so tightly that they remain standing even after the gas has been evacuated, their naked bodies fouled by their last excretion, their faces still gripped by expressions from which life has fled. Like some surrealist tableau. Impossible to assign meaning. More than once Mengele has wanted to clap his hands at this moment, and command them, like Lazarus, to come forth. And more than once, yes, he would swear it, the multitude has trembled on the brink of responding to his thought.

To certify the result, is this to observe? Is this when the mixed state of life and death collapses to its final reality? Pardon, but Mengele doubts it. He would not claim that death can be reversed. But if the quantum universe truly divides at every subatomic transaction, then in other universes death, defeat, and exile can be negated. Undone. The past as well as the future is provisional, in a mixed state awaiting its proper observer. In such a cosmos of eternal possibility, there are no judges. There is no guilt. There is only the flicker of quanta, eternally dancing like Siva at the root of all becoming, deferring all judgment and consequence, yes, to the will of that determined observer who assigns the highest meaning to the experiment.

So although Mengele signs the papers he is not, to his way of thinking, the observer in this situation. The final, intimate task of moving bodies to the crematoria is left to the *Sonder-kommandos*, selected from the prisoners' own ranks. A privileged position: one earns extra food, favors, status. It seems to Mengele that the *Sonderkommandos* are the true observers, entering the chambers after the gas has dispersed, embracing the befouled corpses to separate them one from another, hauling them out, searching body cavities for hidden valuables. Mengele has often watched one particular *Sonderkommando* leader as he delivers his fellows to the furnace, moving like Shadrach unscathed amidst the flames and smoke, surrounded by a black aura of determination more intense than Mengele's own: one of the secret just ones on whom the earth rests. Such a one is the true observer, the true creator of this final reality.

In Serra Negra, a journalist comes to see him under carefully negotiated conditions. Mengele does not admit or deny his identity. The journalist does not press the question. The entire interview has a remote, hypothetical tone, as if Mengele were performing the thought experiment of being Mengele. Do you feel guilt? the journalist asks. To have condemned so many, tortured so many. The question baffles and annoys him. Guilt? You have no conception of the world we could have brought into being. What you call history, what the victors have written, was a mere preliminary. In the ruins of our collapse you see atrocity, and I agree! I agree. But, excuse me, it might have been very different.

After a pause the journalist says —I am Jewish. I am here to try to understand. But you cannot deny or erase the suffering. What you did was an enormous crime, but the crime you meant to accomplish was incomparably greater.

Mengele says —Suffering to no purpose is indeed atrocious. The suffering, say, of old age, which helps no one. But suffering to a purpose is meaningful, even if it is another's purpose. You do not know, says Mengele, thinking of the *Sonderkommando*. Even in Auschwitz there was a sense of shared purpose.

The journalist cuts him off. —Shared? Do you truly suggest that this is the meaning of our suffering? Jews sharing the Nazi purpose?

—What I say is subtle, Mengele begins.

—What you say is abominable, the man says. —You, you who have judged so many, have you no fear of being judged?

—Have you a wallet? Mengele asks. —Show me it.

The journalist looks blank, then shifts a thin haunch and pulls from a rear pocket a worn leather billfold stuffed with papers and cards.

—That is the flayed skin of a horse, says Mengele. —The jew Isaac Bashevis Singer writes, To animals, all men are Nazis.

Mengele never saw what the journalist wrote. Yet the man must have broken his pledge of confidentiality—you could not trust them, ever!—for Mengele heard thereafter of inquiries to Bonn, and so he fled Serra Negra for São Paulo.

Mengele lies atop the bedsheets, an acrid sweat on his white frail limbs. The fly buzzes steadily round the room, turning and turning on random paths.

If we are mere collections of unresolved possibilities, under the eye of some final determiner, how can we know if our very consciousness is true or false? How can we know, even, that we live? Perhaps, though we think ourselves alive, we are dead, and unaware of it. If so, when did our consciousness begin to deceive us? If we exist in a mixed state, the only certainty is non-existence before and after; all else is illusion. Birth itself is a deception, death the corrective.

And if consciousness deceives, then death, the liberation, can be conferred only by an observer. This was the revelation that he, *schöne Josef*, had brought like an angel to all the jews who had waited so long for their messiah. He, not the *Sonderkommando*, is one of the secret just ones, who after all this time has realized the true and highest meaning, that no matter how long or cleverly deferred, the final outcome of the atrocious experiment of life never varies.

The fly bumbles against the ceiling. Above it the jew in his cell is getting to his feet and looking around, as though able for the first time to see outside his cell. The jew *observes* Mengele. Never in his life has Mengele quailed from the eyes of another person, but he quails now. The jew is more real than the room, the tired afternoon sunlight, the grime on the window, and Mengele is unable to look away from his burning eyes. They are the eyes of Martin Buber, of Hannah Arendt, of the journalist, of the *Sonderkommando*, of a gypsy child. They are six million lives. Not suspended, not mixed, not reclaimable by some jesuitical parsing of the atom, but lost beyond recall.

Stop it! cries Mengele. You are finished, all of you! I have sentenced the entire jewish race to death! You live only in my mind! It is I who assign meaning! I! He raises his arm to sweep the vision aside, and knocks the volume of Martin Buber onto the trap. The steel arm slams down, and the canister arcs through the air, bangs against the locked door. Gas erupts into the room. Mengele struggles out of bed, but his legs will not support him, and as he staggers and falls he hears a rush of music, *alle Menschen werden Brüder*, as the final determination descends upon him and carries him into the universal fraternity of death.

THE AMOUNT TO CARRY

Et la Splendide-Hôtel fut bâti dans le chaos de glaces et de nuit du pôle.

—RIMBAUD

THE LEGAL secretary of the Workman's Accident Insurance Institute for the Kingdom of Bohemia in Prague enters the atrium of the hotel. Slender, sickly, his tall frame seems bowed under the weight of his title. But his dark darting eyes, in a boyish face as pale as milk, take in the scene eagerly.

What a fantastic place! The dream of a visionary American, the hotel has been under construction since the end of the War. A brochure lists its many firsts: an observatory, a radio station, a resident orchestra (Arnold Schönberg conducting), an indoor health spa, bank kiosks open day and night for currency exchange. From the atrium an escalator carries guests to the mezzanine, where a strange aeroplane is suspended, naked as a bicycle, like something designed by da Vinci or a Cro-Magnon, nothing like the machines the secretary saw at the Brescia air show, years ago.

The secretary likes hotels. He loses himself in their depths,

their receding corridors, the chiming of lifts, the jangle of tele-
phones, the thump of pneumatic tubes. It is the freedom of
anonymity, with roast duck and dumplings on the side.

A placard in the lobby proclaims in four languages, *Conference
of International Insurance Executives—Registration*. Europe has gone
mad for conferences. More placards welcome rocketeers, phi-
losophers, alpinists, and the Catholic Total Abstinence Union.
So many conferences are underway that the crowd seems
formed of smaller crowds, intersecting, breaking apart, and reforming on their ways to meetings, meals, or diversions, jostling
like bemused fowl.

The falsity of public places. Their implacable reality.

Hotels he likes, but not conferences. His first was eight years
ago. Terrified beyond stage fright, he spoke on accident pre-
vention in the workplace. He felt sure that the men listening
would fall on him and tear him apart when they understood
what he was saying. But he was wrong. They recognized that
with safer conditions fewer claims would be filed. With a law-
yer's cunning the secretary had put altruism before them as self-
interest. He felt such relief as he left the stage that he was unable
to stay for the other talks. Uncontrollable laughter welled up in
him as he bolted for the door.

That was 1913, the year his first book was published. Now,
at thirty-eight, he is becoming known for his writing, but finds
himself miserably unable to write. Summoned to the castle but
kept at the gate. And his time grows short. Last month at
Matliary he underwent another hopeless treatment. It rained the
whole time. At the end of his stay the weather cleared, and he
hiked in the mountains. On his return, Prague seemed more
oppressive than the sanatorium. Some dybbuk of the perverse
made him volunteer for the conference.

The secretary pauses at a display of models. Marvels of America, of engineering. New York City! Finely carved ships are

afloat in a harbor of blue sand. Pasteboard cliffs rise from the sand, buildings and spires surmount the island. In the harbor stands a crowned green female, Liberty, tall as a building, holding aloft a sword.

Beyond a glass terrace is the hotel's deer park, an immense enclosed courtyard. On its grass peacocks stride, tails dragging. One turns to face him. The iridescent blue of its chest. The pitiless black stones of its eyes.

The sideboard in his suite holds fresh flowers, a bottle of champagne, a bowl of oranges, a telephone. From his window he sees a lake and thinks of Palestine.

The gentleman from Hartford pauses at the cigar stand. A wooden Indian shades its eyes against the sun of an imaginary prairie. The gentleman purchases a panatela. Bold type on a magazine arrests his eye: *de stijl.* Opening it he reads, *The object of this magazine will be to contribute to the development of a new consciousness of beauty.* On the facing page is a photograph of this very hotel. Beauty. Is that what surrounds him? He looks from the photo of the lobby into the lobby. He adds the magazine and a Paris *Herald* to his purchase, receiving in change a bright 1920 American dime. His wife, Elsie, regards him sidelong from its face.

Crowds rush to their morning appointments. Mr Stevens is free until lunch. In truth, his presence here is unnecessary to his agency's business, but he has developed a knack of absences from home and from his wife.

His attention is taken by a scale model of the hotel itself, accurate even to the construction scaffolding over the entrance. Through a tiny window of the tiny penthouse he sees two figures studying blueprints unfurled between them.

In *de stijl*, Stevens reads: Like the young century itself, the hotel is a vortex of energies and styles. It thrusts upward, sprawls sideways, even sends an arm into the lake, where a floating walkway winds through a houseboat colony designed by Frank Lloyd Wright, fresh from his triumphant Imperial Hotel in Tokyo. Many architects have been engaged, Gropius and Le Corbusier, de Klerk and Mendelsohn; they draw up plans, begin work, are dismissed or quit; so the hotel itself remains more an idea than a thing, a series of sketches of itself, a diffracted view not unlike M. Duchamp's notorious *Nude* in the New York Armory Show of some years ago. The hotel is a sort of manifesto-in-progress to a multiple futurism, as though the very idea of the modern is too energetic and protean to find a single unified expression.

It occurs to Stevens that the hotel is unreal. Reality is an exercise of the most august imagination. This place is a hodge-podge. It gives him a sense of his own unreality. Then again, the real world seen by an imaginative man may very well seem like an imaginative construction.

He folds the magazine and looks for a place to smoke in peace.

The senior partner of Ives & Myrick awakes right early. The morning light is somehow wrong. And where is Harmony, his wife? Outside, birds sing their dawn chorus, hitting all the notes between the notes. He remembers the two pianos in the Sunday school room of Central Presbyterian. One piano had fallen a quartertone flat of the other. He tried out chords on the two of them at once, right hand on one, left hand on the other. Notes between notes—an infinity of notes! Again and again he struck those splendid new chords. Out of tune—what an idea! Can the universe be out of tune?

Now he remembers. The conference. It should be Mike Myrick here. He's better at this hail-fellow-well-met stuff. But

Mike said Ives should go. Do you a world of good, Charlie. Write some music on the boat. Give Harmony some time off from you. Ives had been laid up for three months after his second heart attack. It wore Harmony out, caring for him. Mike's right, she deserves a vacation from him.

These memory lapses worry him. He's forty-seven years old, he calls in sick a lot, he's not pulling his weight. His job, his future, how long can he keep it up? Shy Charlie, who's never sold a policy in his life, has come to this conference to prove the point—to himself, he guesses—that he's still an asset to the agency, and no loafer.

Out of bed, then. On the desk is the latest draft of his essay, "The Amount to Carry," condensed for his luncheon talk. Just the key points. It is at once a mathematical formula for estate planning and a practical guide to making the sale. Sell to the masses! Get into the lives of the people! I can answer scientifically the one essential question. Do you know what that is?

In the last twelve years Ives & Myrick has taken in two hundred million dollars. Two millions of that have gone to Ives. By any measure he's a rich man, but still he dreads retirement. The end of his usefulness, of his strength. So he's making provisions. Much of his income now comes from renewal commissions. Normally the selling agent gets a nice piece of change every time a policy is renewed, but that takes years, and the younger men are impatient, so they've been selling their commissions to him at a discount. A little irregular, perhaps, but they're happy to take the money!

A man has to provide for his family. They adopted Edie five years ago, and her parents still ask for help. It amounts to buying the child. But isn't Edie better off now? When Harmony lost their baby, she and Charlie wept nightlong. For a month she lay in hospital. Sick with despair and worry, Charlie set to music a Keats poem:

The spirit is too weak;
mortality weighs heavily upon me
like unwilling sleep,
and each imagined pinnacle and steep
tells me I must die,
like a sick eagle looking towards the sky.

From that day he knew that they must carry one another. It scared him, then, for two people to so depend.

The money's for his music too. It cost him two thousand dollars last year to print the "Concord" Sonata. And it will cost a sight more to bring out the songs. But the only way the lily boys and the Rollos will ever hear this music is if he prints it himself. He mailed seven hundred copies of the "Concord" to names culled from *Who's Who* and the *Musical Courier*'s subscription list. Gave offense to several musical pussies. All those nice Mus Docks and ladybirds falling over in a faint at the sight of his manly dissonances.

In open rehearsal last spring the respected conductor Paul Eisler, holding a nice baton, led his New Symphony through Ives's "Decoration Day." Musicians dropped out one by one, till by the last measure a violinist in the back row was the sole survivor. There is a limit to musicianship, said Eisler coldly, handing the score back to Ives.

A limit to someone's, anyway.

But this fuss with revisions and printers is hollow. The truth is he hasn't written any new music since his illness—since the War, really. If music is through with him, he guesses he can take it, he's written enough. But how do you get it heard? Isn't it enough to write it? Do you have to carry it on your back into the town square?

Wilson dead and the League of Nations with him. That weak sister Harding in the White House.

He's getting into one of his black moods that Harmony so hates, and he'd better not, not with his talk ahead of him. He saw a piano in a room off the main lobby. Playing it might put him right.

When the secretary was hired in 1908, the Institute was a scandal, not unlike the life insurance companies in New York a few years earlier, though it was a scandal of Bohemian incompetence rather than American greed. For twenty years the Institute had run at a loss. The secretary's hiring coincided with a sweeping reform. He was made to put a cash value on various injuries: lost limbs, fingers, hands, toes, eyes, and other maimings. He adjusted premiums, which had been constant, to correspond to levels of risk in specific occupations. In the course of travel to verify claims, he found himself examining production methods and machinery. Once he even redesigned a mechanical planer to make it safer.

Even the most cautious worker is drawn into the cutting space when the cutter slips or the lumber is thrown back, which happens often. . . . Accidents usually take off several finger joints or whole fingers.

How modest these people are. Instead of storming the Institute and smashing the place to bits, they come and plead.

The gentleman from Hartford locates an armchair. At one end of the bronze-trimmed parlor stands a potted palm, in which a mechanical bird twitters silently. The dime is still in his hand. Surely she is beautiful: Elsie in a Phrygian cap, the Roman symbol of a freed slave. The master carving by Adolph Weinman, twelve inches across, is on their mantelpiece. Does Stevens oppress her? Does Weinman think so, is that the message of the cap? Its wings court confusion with Mercury, Hermes, messen-

ger, god of merchants and thieves, patron of eloquence and
fraud. Holder of the caduceus, whose touch makes gold. On
the reverse, a bundle of sticks, Roman fasces. He tucks the coin
into a vest pocket, feeling his ample flesh yield beneath the
cloth. That monster, the body.

He unfolds the *Herald*. Victor Emmanuel III is losing power
to blackshirted anarchists called *fascisti*. The Paris Peace Conference demands 132 billion gold marks in reparations from Germany, prompting a violent protest from the new chairman of
the National Socialist German Workers' Party, some berber with
a Chaplin-Hardy mustache. European politics is *opera buffa*,
when not *bruta*. Stevens turns with relief to the arts section.
New Beethoven biography by Thayer. New music festival in
Donaueschingen. Caruso still being mourned. Play by Karel Ca-
pek, *R.U.R.*, opens in Prague. Review of Van Vechten's new
book.

Lately Van Vechten suggested Stevens assemble a book of
poems. He promised to give it personally to Alfred Knopf.
Surely it's time for his first book, whatever friction it causes
with Elsie. Stevens is forty-two.

At the Arensbergs' once, Elsie said, *I like Mr Stevens's writing
when it is not affected. But it is so often affected.* No, what she
liked was being his sole reader. When he sent poems out she
resented it.

He unrings the panatela, rolling it between his fingers as he
turns titles in his mind. *Supreme Fiction. The Grand Poem: Preliminary Minutiæ.* How little it would take to turn poets into the
only true comedians.

As he's about to light up, a sobersided balding type sits at the
piano. New York suit, Yankee set to his jaw. After a moment
he starts to play plain chords, as from a harmonium in a country
church. Stevens thinks he knows the hymn from his Lutheran
childhood, but then there are wrong notes and false harmonies,
played not with the hesitations and corrections of an amateur,

but with steady confidence. A pianist himself, Stevens listens closely. At an anacrusis, the treble disjoints from the bass and goes its own way, in another key and another time. His listening mind is both enchanted and repelled. Music then is feeling, not sound.

A tall thin Jew with jug ears and a piercing gaze, *echt mitteleuropisch*, has paused in the doorway to hear the Yankee's fantasia.

—*Doch, dass kenn' ich,* he says.

The Yankee starts, but says nothing.

—That, that music you play. In München war's, *vor zehn Jahren. Mit Max Brod bin ich zu einem Konzert gegangen. Mahler dirigierte. Diese Melodien, genau so.*

—Huh? says the Yankee.

—Something about a concert, Stevens interjects from his chair, startling Ives again. —He says he's heard that song before. At a concert in Munich ten years ago. Conducted by Mahler.

—Gustav Mahler?

—*Ja ja, Gustav Mahler! Ich erinnere mich ganz klar. Am Schluss klangen die Glocken, gleichzeitig spielte etwas vollkommen anderes in den Streichern. Unheimlich* war's.

—He says a bell part, against strings at the end, in, apparently, two different keys?

—Yes! That's it! *Glocken* and *Streicher*! The Yankee's German is atrocious.

—*Glock*en, agrees the Jew. —*Ganz unheimlich.*

—An uncanny effect, says Stevens.

—But that's my Third Symphony! How could he have heard it? It's never been performed. Tams, my copyist, he once told me that Mahler came looking for American scores. This was in 'ten, when Mahler conducted the New York Phil. Tams said he took my Third. I never believed it, I thought Tams lost the score and made up a tale. But by God, it must be true!

The Yankee, excited now and voluble, rises from the piano

bench, extending a hand. —Charles Ives, Ives & Myrick Agency, New York. Life insurance.

—Franz Kafka. Of Workman's Accident Insurance Institute in Praha. I am very pleased to meet you.

—Cough . . . ?

—Kafka.

Stevens, having unwisely involved himself, cannot now politely withdraw to the solitary pleasure of his cigar.

—Stevens, Hartford Casualty. Surety bonds.

—Hartford? says Ives. —We used to have an office in Hartford. Are you a Yale man?

—Harvard '01.

—Yale '98, says Ives, defensively.

—Do you live in New York, Mr Ives?

—New York and Redding.

—Reading! Pennsylvania?

—Redding Connecticut.

—Oh, Redding. I'm from Reading Pennsylvania.

—I thought you said Hartford.

—I was born in Reading. As was my wife.

—My wife Harmony's a Hartford girl. Her father is the Reverend Joe Twitchell. He's the man that married and buried Mark Twain.

—I've heard of Twain, says Stevens drily.

—A great American writer, says Kafka.

—Are you married, Mr Kavka? asks Ives.

—Married . . . no. An elderly . . . bachelor, do you say? With a bad habit of, ah, *Verlobungen*? Engagements?

Ives appears shocked by this display of loose European mores, and Stevens hastens to change the subject.

—Mr Ives, do you happen to know Edgard Varèse?

—Who?

—A composer. He moved to Greenwich Village from Paris. He founded the New Symphony a few years ago.

Ives narrows his eyes. —Never heard of him. Some Bohemian city slicker, I guess.

—Bohemian? asks Kafka.

—Meaning an artistic type, says Stevens. —*La vie bohême.* Are
you artistic, Herr Kafka?

The faint smile on Kafka's face vanishes. Dismay fills his serious dark eyes.

—Oh, not in the least.

Ives strides briskly to the luncheon. He's keyed up, excited,
raring to go. He took to the hotel at once, its brash mix of
styles, chrome and ormolu, like a clamor of Beethoven, church
hymns, and camp marches. He passes the scale model of Manhattan, so finely made he can almost pick out the Ives & Myrick
office on Liberty Street. But what is this? South and east of
Central Park are two unfamiliar needletopped skyscrapers, taller
even than the Woolworth Building. The downtown building is
where the Waldorf-Astoria should be. Surely that's not right, yet
something about them projects a natural authority. As he puz-
zles, he hears a shout.

—Fire!

People turn. Ives smells smoke. A clerk steps forward.

—Please! No cause for concern! There is always a fire somewhere in the hotel. We have the most modern sprinkler and
containment systems. Everything is under control.

And indeed, the smoke has dispersed. Guests return to their
occupations.

At luncheon, Stevens is seated across from Kafka. Kafka slides
his *veau cordon bleu*, fatted calf, to one side of the plate and
diligently chews some green beans. Stevens is looking on with,
he realizes as Kafka's penetrating gaze meets his, the jaundiced

eye that Oliver Hardy turns on Stan Laurel. Stevens touches his
ginger mustache and looks away. Ives is holding forth to the
luncheon.

—Life insurance is doing its part in the progress of the greater
life values.

Stevens, on his third glass of Haut-Medoc, cocks an eyebrow
at the podium. Can Ives believe this stuff? Has he forgotten the
Armstrong Act? Just fifteen years ago, the life insurance business
was so corrupt that even the New York legislature couldn't ignore it. Sales commissions were fifty, eighty, one hundred percent of the premiums. Executive parties were bacchanals.
Mutual president Richard McCurdy, before his indictment,
called life insurance "a great benevolent missionary institution".
His own benevolence had enriched his family by fifteen millions. The state shut down half the agencies and sent any number of executives into forced retirement. Come to think of it,
that's probably how young Ives got his start, stepping into that
vacuum.

As a surety claims attorney, Stevens is inclined to finical
doubt. Defaults, breaches, and frauds are his profession. He is a
rabbi of the ways and means by which people evade their com-
mitments and excuse themselves. He feels that the attempt to
secure one's interests against chance and fate is noble but vain.
Insurance is a communal project but a capitalist enterprise, a
compassionate ideal ruled by the equations of actuaries. In the
risk pool, it may appear that the fortunate succor the misfor-
tunate, but that is a salesman's fiction; the pool is more like a
mass of gas molecules in Herr Boltzmann's kinetic theory. The
position of the individual is unimportant. We are dust in the
wind. What can we insure?

Kafka is still chewing.

Insurance is only the prelude to Ives's fugue: now he is off
onto nationwide town meetings, referenda, the will of the peo-

ple, the majority! Quotations from Shakespeare, Lamb, Emerson, Thoreau. He's lost his audience.

From a tablemate, Stevens hears, —Deny a claim for a year and most people give up.

Stevens feels a fleeting pang for Ives's pure, unreal belief. The poet chides himself: Have it your way. The world is ugly, and the people are sad.

The final belief is to believe in a fiction which you know to be a fiction, because there is nothing else.

After his talk, Ives is depressed and uncertain. His exhilirations are often followed by a crash. He doubts that he put over any of it, apart from the business formulas. Yet surely, after the War, after the Spanish influenza that swept the globe, all men must see that their common good is one.

The fabric of existence weaves itself whole. His music and his business are not separate; his talk was as pure an expression of his belief and will as any of his music. He's given it his best, and now he has no interest for the rest of the proceedings. He's ready to go home. He leaves behind the meeting rooms overfull with conventioneers, passes vacant ballrooms with distant ceilings, he walks down deserted corridors where the repeating patterns of carpet, the drift of dust in afternoon sun, are desolate with melancholy, ennui, loss. It begins to frighten him, this vast, unfathomable place. He is overcome with a sense of futility. He thinks of his father's band playing gavottes at the battle of Chancellorsville.

Turning a corner, he spots the one-legged concierge, limping and clanking down the hall. The old rogue comes right up to Ives.

—I carry about in my belt sixteen thousand francs in gold. It weighs over eight kilos and gives me dysentery.

—Why do you carry it? asks Ives, caught off guard.

—For my art! To insure my liberty. Soon I will have enough!

—I see. Can you tell me the way to the main lobby?

Scornfully the ancient laughs. —You see nothing. That way.

The elevator lurches to a halt between floors.

There are numbers between numbers, thinks Stevens. Between the integers are fractions, and between those the irrationals, and so on to the dust of never-quite-continuity. If numerical continuity is an illusion, perhaps temporal continuity is as well. Perhaps there are dark nothings between our flickers of consciousness, as between the frames of a movie. The Nude of Duchamp descends her staircase in discrete steps. Where is she between steps? Perhaps here at the hotel. At this moment, stuck between floors, where am I?

Stevens presses the button for ROOF. The elevator begins to move sideways.

Past its glass doors windows glide horizontally by, offering views of the city, shrunk to insignificance by height. The car seems to be traveling along the circumference of a tower. After a quarter circuit, the car resumes ascent.

Its doors open to verdancy. The rooftop garden is a maze, a forest, an artificial world. A hothouse opens onto an arcade that corners into an arbor. Lemon thyme grows between the cobbles. He crushes fragrance as he walks. In his more virile youth, he often hiked thirty miles in a day up the Hudson from New York, or ferried to New Jersey to ramble through the open country near Hackensack, Englewood, Hohokus. Slowly he finds a geography in the paths, steps, and terraces. It is indeed a world. Small signs, like lexical weeds, mark frontiers. From SOUTH AMERICA and its spiked succulents with their starburst flowers of yellow and pink and blue he enters MEXICO. On the path is a fallen *tomato verde*. The enclosing lantern, which the fruit has not quite grown to fill, is purple at the stem and papery, but at the tip has decayed to a tough, brittle lace of veins, like an autumn leaf. Inside the small green fruit is split. His fingers come away gummy.

Abruptly, past espaliered pears, there is the roofedge, cantilevered into space. Light scatters through the atoms of the air: blue. Not even sky is continuous.

Distant snowcapped peaks shelve off into sky. He remembers with sharp yearning his camping and hunting trip in British Columbia with Peckham and their rough guides. Twenty years ago. Another lost paradise.

His elate melancholy follows the ups and downs of the distant range: however long he lives, how much and well he writes, no poetry can compass this world, the actual.

K decides to walk in the city, but the hotel baffles his efforts to leave it. Corridors lead past ballrooms and parlors, but never reach the atrium. After ten minutes, K stops at a desk in an arcade.

—*Bitte, wie geht man hinaus?*

—And why do you want to go out?

Though the desk clerk has clearly understood K's question, he answers in English, and with another question. K is annoyed, but perseveres in German.

—*Ich will spazieren gehn.*

—You can walk in the hotel. Try the lake ramp, the deer park, the rooftop gardens. Here is a map.

—*Danke nein.*

K turns down corridors at random. At the end of one he sees sunlight. Although the exit door is marked CLOSED UNDER CONSTRUCTION it is unlocked. He transgresses and finds himself in a small grotto, perhaps a corner of the deer park. Around him the hotel walls rise sixteen floors to a cantilevered roof.

He is in a graveyard of worn stones. His fingers move right to left over the nearest. *Beautiful eldest, rest in peace, Anshel Mor Henach. 5694 Sivan 3.*

The gentleman from Hartford has dined alone. Susceptible with wine he follows the chance of shifting crowds through the lobby.

—*Faites vos jeux, mesdames messieurs.*

The casino's Doric columns remind Stevens of the Hartford office. A temple to probability, and the profit to be had from it.

Dice chatter, balls racket round their polished course, cards slap and sigh on baize. In his good ear rings the bright syrinx of hazard. In the bad one, the dull hoo-hoo of drums. Chance and fate, high flute and groaning bass.

—*Un coup de dés jamais n'abolira le hasard.*

Stevens bets. The wheel rumbles, the ball rattles.

In the spa, K glimpses himself in a full length mirror. Hollow cheeks, sunken stomach, spindly legs, ribs like a charcoal sketch of famine. Other nude bodies, ghostly in steam, pass in a line. In modesty he turns away, but he sees then uniformed men, like guards in some Strafkolonie, herding the others through doors. The flesh of their bodies is as haggard as their faces. The men are all circumcised. Then come the women. Faces downcast, but some turn to him.

—*Ottla! Elli! Valli!*

Is there no end to this? Another woman turns her imploring face to him.

—*Milena!*

The doors close, and he is alone but for two guards murmuring in German, the angelic tongue of Goethe and Kleist. K is invisible to them. Their gleaming leather boots, their gray uniforms, the stark black and white device on their red armbands, show none of the Prussian love of pomp. This is something new. Yet it is the old story.

Enough, then! Let it be done! Let every child of Israel be run through the Harrow and tattooed with the name of his crime: *Jude.* All but K the invisible, the impervious. Instead of him they have taken Milena, not even a Jew, for the crime of having loved him.

The vision passes. K dresses, slowly apprehending that the hotel is not style, but a force as implacable as history. He has lived through one world war and will not live to see another. But unlike Ives with his one-world utopianism, unlike Stevens in the protected precincts of his being, K knows that another war is coming.

Style is optional, history is not.

In his room that night, Ives tries to compose.

Six years past, in the Adirondacks, he had a vision of earth, mountains, and sky as music. In the predawn it seemed that he was high above the earth, Keene Valley stretched below him, mist lying in its sinuous watercourse and the lights of the town burning within it like coals in smoke. The last stars were fading, and the horizon held bands of rose, orange, and indigo. The greening forests took on color and depth, the fallow fields, the curdling mist. He imagined several orchestras, huge conclaves of singing men and women, placed in valleys, on hillsides, on mountain tops. The universe in tones, or a Universe Symphony.

The plan still terrifies him. He's made notes and sketches, but the real work hasn't begun. He doubts he can do it. The vision is remote now, a fading memory, impalpable as his childhood. He sits, he sketches, he notes. Even at this hour from some far part of the hotel the sound of construction is unceasing.

Danbury and Redding seem another world. He no longer knows how things go together.

Pulmonary edema due to arteriosclerotic and hypertensive heart disease with probable myocardial infarction.

He sees an old man outside the house in Redding. An airplane buzzes overhead, and the old man shakes his cane at it. The hillsides and valleys roll away into the haze of distance. It's all there, the old man thinks. If only I could have done it.

Sleepless, K sits writing to Max, to Klopstock, to his sisters Elli and Ottla. He starts and tears up another letter to Milena. What is left to say?

His windows are black as a peacock's eyes. Memory is a pyre that burns forever. Felice, Grete, Milena, how shamefully he has treated them.

The life one lives and the stories one tells about it are never the same. Every moment has a secret narrative, so intertwined with those of other moments that finding the truth about anything becomes a labor of Zeno. An endless maze of connecting tunnels, branching and intersecting without end.

He sips at a glass of water, swallows with difficulty.

Laryngologische Klinik

Pat.-Nr. 135

Name: Dr Kafka Franz

Diagnose: Tbc. laryngis

Pat. ist völlig appetitlos u. fühlt sich sehr schwach.

Pupillen normal, reagieren prompt.

Pat. ist leicht heiser.

Hinterwand infiltriert.

Taschenbänder gerötet.

Haemsputum.

What is it, to write? I want rather to live.

He will give Milena all his diaries. Let her see what he is, let her take him entire. Is this contrition? Or a sly way of freeing himself from his burden? Or is it, at last, the only marriage he can make?

A curious small voice addresses the secretary: *It was late in the evening when K arrived. The village was deep in snow.* He holds the pen unmoving.

A faint squeaking comes from the floor. Near the head of the bed is a mousehole, from which a small gray head peers. A pink nose winks at him.

—*Guten Abend, Fräulein Maus.* What a pretty voice, what a singer you are! Won't you come in? Come, here is a nice warm slipper to sleep in.

He edges his foot forward, slipper on his toe. Whiskers twitch and the mouse is gone, running in the tiny corridor behind the baseboard, through all the secret passages of the hotel, un-watched, unsuspected, secure.

It is late. The model Manhattan is now a cordillera of skyscrap-ers. At the island's southmost tip rise a pair of silver towers, blunt as commerce. Stevens feels old, past meridian. His own worldliness reproves him. He understands nothing of the cold wind and polar night in which he moves. But he knows that he will live through awful silences to old age.

There is no insurance. There is no liberty. Elsie is his wife, despite his yes her no. He must be better to her.

The airplane has come and gone. The Redding air is still. He listens to the silence: his blood thrums, a jackdaw cries, wind rustles an oak. Universe symphony. And Edith calls, running towards him:

—Daddy! Carry me!

He catches her up and lifts her onto his shoulders. Her thin legs dangle down.

—Carry me! she commands again, and he starts towards the house, where Harmony has stepped onto the porch. She sees them, and the moment is so full that he pauses under Edie's weight, misses his step, then quickly recovers, walking forward as Harmony calls in concern:

—Charlie! Your heart!

From uneasy dreams the secretary awakens transformed. A coverlet recedes before him like the Alps. He holds out his hands, seeing spindly shanks, thin gray fur, grasping claws. There comes a heavy knock at the door. He scampers across the bed, his claws grasping the fabric as he goes down the side and under the bed. Cowering there, nose twitching, chest heaving, tail wrapped round his shivering flanks, he sees the enormous legs of the maid moving about the room. She is sweeping with a broom as big as a house. Crumbs fly past him like stones. In a storm of dust he sneezes and trembles.

Near the head of the bed he spies the dark hole in the baseboard, and without a moment's thought he dashes for it. The maid exclaims, the shadow of the broom descends, he is squeaking in terror, running, and then he is in his burrow, in the darkness, in the walls of the hotel, carrying nothing, but wearing, as it were, the whole world.